JOSIAH

Jason Potter

Unsubscribe Publishing

For my amazing wife Rachelle and my four awesome children, Hannah, Jonathan, Jessica, and William.

For Mrs. McGinn

And for the childhood friends who helped me overcome my loneliness, Louise T, Paul D, Ben S and Anna D.

CONTENTS

PREFACE

It was an overcast day, the wet and cold atmosphere making it one of those dreary days that seem like they will never end. Most of the students had stopped listening to Mrs. West already; we were just waiting for the lunch period.

Finally, the bell sounded, and the whole class rushed out the door. The wind made me shiver as I made my way out of the classroom and headed towards the canteen for lunch.

Buying lunch was a rare privilege during those days. Mum usually packed me a frozen Vegemite-and-cheese sandwich that would be made a few weeks in advance. She'd give it to me every day straight out of the freezer, and it would thaw in my lunchbox every morning. But today was one of those special days when Mum had run out of sandwiches and had a few spare coins so I could buy lunch at school.

The canteen was on the other side of the school

from our grade-six classroom, so the lucky ones among us started to head towards the canteen. It was also where cola-flavoured Sunny Boys and all the lollies that we could afford awaited us.

As I took my usual shortcut to the canteen, right between the admin building and the library, I felt two hands grab me from behind. They pinned my arms behind my back and held on tight while someone roped something around my neck.

I kicked my left leg backwards and tried to free my arms, but their hold wouldn't loosen up. A sinking feeling of panic swirled in my stomach, swimming through my veins, muscles, and right up my throat, where a wire was being tightened dangerously. The utter panic and fear made me freeze up and locked my body in place. I could hear their loud, taunting laughter in my ears as I began to thrash my arms back and forth in a fight to save myself.

This experience and others just like it left me frightened and fearful, and while my story begins much earlier, these attacks, when I was a target for others, could have defined my life if I let them.

1

In the Beginning

I was born in 1972 in Port Lincoln, a small country town on the coast of South Australia. My father worked for the South Australian government, giving support and advice to local farmers in the district. My mum worked as a nurse before I was born, but once I came along, she looked after our home and helped other families in our community as well. Every Sunday, we would head off to church, where Mum and Dad were often involved, helping run the service, providing morning tea or lunch as well.

My father's job required him to move to a different town every year or two, so my family moved around a lot in those early years. My mum grew up in a rural town in South Australia, while my dad was born and raised in Adelaide—a city boy who loved the outdoors. He grew up in a conservative family with parents who loved him but were very strict. On the other hand, my mum had parents who were separated, so she was mainly raised by her sister and her dad.

My story begins with some of my earliest memories. From a very young age, I learned by trying something out first and thinking about what might happen afterwards.

One of my earliest memories is a great example of exactly this kind of thinking. Our family had a thin, brown bookcase that leaned against the wall of the lounge room. All I remember thinking was, *I wonder if I could climb that?*

I waddled over to it, reached up with my right hand, and began to climb it. I put my left hand on the same shelf as my right hand and then lifted my right leg off the ground and began to climb. As I lifted my left leg off the ground, I felt the bookcase wobble a bit, and I remember feeling nervous for a second, but I pressed on. It was a stretch to get from the bottom shelf to the next one, but I was determined, and I went through the same steps, right hand on the next shelf, then left hand, right leg up, and then left leg.

I put my left leg up onto the next shelf, and I just froze. The bookcase was moving! I looked up and could see the top of the bookcase slowly moving away from the wall. The bookcase gathered speed, and the books began to fall out of the shelves as I headed backwards towards the floor. There was a tremendous crash, and I landed flat on my back with books everywhere and the bookcase on top of me, trapping me underneath. I yelled and yelled and yelled, but it seemed like ages before Mum found me. She came running into the lounge room, lifted up the bookcase, pulled me out in one quick movement, and gave me a huge hug.

"Are you okay? Are you hurt?" she asked.

I couldn't really speak. I was shaking all over; I got such a fright. Mum just held me until I calmed down and began to relax.

A couple of years later, our family moved to Mount Gambier, a rural town in South Australia. Mount Gambier was like many towns in the mid-1970s, with a thriving agricultural industry that supported its economy, as well as a couple of tourist attractions, the most famous being a blue lake and some incredible caves. My parents packed up all our belongings into tea chests at our old house on the coast, the mover packed the truck, and off we went for the three-hour drive to our new hometown.

When we arrived at the new house, my younger brother Matt and I were left to explore the garage and the yard while the movers unpacked our belongings from their truck. As I looked around the new house and checked it out, I decided I did not like it. In fact, I was very unimpressed. I hated this new house, and I wanted to go back to the old one.

I waited and watched till my tricycle was unpacked. I called Matt over. "I can't stand this place," I said to him. "Let's get out of here and go back to our old house." Matt didn't really talk much, but he didn't argue when I picked him up and put him on back half of the tricycle seat.

The gate at the end of the driveway was open, so I rode to the end of the driveway with Matt holding on tight and turned left to go back to the old house we just came from. What I didn't find out till much later was we were heading off in the wrong direction!

I had no idea how long this would take, but I was certain my parents had made a terrible mistake, and if we headed back to the old house, they would change their mind and come too. I rode the tricycle to the end of the street and turned right to go back the way I thought we had come. The footpath was all grass, so I rode on the road because I couldn't turn the pedals on the grass with Matt on the back; the wheels sank into the dirt too much. The white line in the middle of the road seemed to go in the right direction, so I headed towards it to follow it back to our old house.

By the time Mum and Dad noticed we weren't around, we were well out of sight. I think they were so busy organising all the furniture and boxes, we left without them spotting us.

Dad told me later that he and Mum came outside to find us and see if Matt and I wanted any morning tea, only to find that we were gone. Mum and Dad looked around the front and back yards, down the driveway and into the street, but we were nowhere to be seen. So, they jumped in their car and began searching.

I was determined to get back to our old place. So, on we went, following the white lines straight down the middle of the road. A car went past and honked the horn. I didn't wave, though. I was worried what would happen if I took my hand off the handlebars. I didn't want to fall off with Matt on the back of the tricycle. Another car came up fast and then slowed down as it went past us. The road we were on had gutters now and a footpath on the side, but I was only interested in following the white lines. A couple of people called out to us, but I ignored them and kept going.

Suddenly, a car drove right up to us and stopped right next to our tricycle. The door opened, and out jumped Dad from the driver's seat. He looked very upset. He didn't say anything; he just opened the back door, picked me and Matt up off our tricycle, and plonked us on the back seat of the car. Mum was sitting in the passenger seat and looked like she had been crying. She looked around and asked me, "What were you doing?"

"Going back to our old house," I said. It seemed to me to be the most obvious thing in the world. Why else would we be riding back where we came from? By this time, Dad had put the tricycle in the boot and was getting into the driver's seat. He patted Mum on the shoulder and looked around at us.

"What on earth were you doing riding in the middle of the road?" he thundered.

"I was following the white lines back to our old

house," I stammered, as my confidence began to ebb away. Dad turned around and mumbled something to Mum I couldn't hear, started the car, and began to drive us back to our new house. I think I freaked them out pretty good.

Our new home ended up being quite memorable. It had a hallway with a kitchen at the end, and the entrance to the house was about halfway down the hallway. This was perfectly designed for a game I used to play with Mum. I would start running from one end of the hallway towards the kitchen, where I jumped up in the air, and my mum would always catch me. We played this game almost every day while my dad was at work.

One afternoon, my dad came home from work, and I decided to play this game with him. He was standing at the end of the hallway in the kitchen, talking to my mum, and I started running towards them. Knowing that my dad would catch me instead of my mum this time, I ran faster and called out, "Dad, Dad, Dad," as I ran. I jumped into the air with all my might. As I jumped up high and floated gracefully through the air (or so I imagined), my dad turned away from me towards the kitchen, and I went flying past him, frantically waving my arms in an attempt to stop myself.

I hit my head on the cupboards on the other side of the kitchen, splitting my head open on the door handle – one of those 1970s circular handles, a bit hollow in the middle but edgier on the outside. As I lay on the floor, I could feel this tremendous pain. I put my hand on my forehead, and my hand was wet. I had split my head open just above my left eye, and there was blood everywhere. I couldn't really see properly because the blood was coming down over my eyes.

I heard my dad say, "What did he do that for?" I was crying and thinking over and over, *Why didn't he catch me?* Mum explained the game to Dad while they grabbed a towel to put on my head to stop the bleeding. "We had better take him to the doctor," said Dad. "I can't stop the bleeding." So, they wrapped a towel around my head and carried me hurriedly out to the car to go to the doctor. Dad drove the car while Mum sat with me in the back seat.

The doctor was a bit surprised when he heard the story, but he cleaned me up, and I ended up with three stiches just to the right side of my left eyebrow. The stiches made me look like a pirate, which I thought was pretty cool, and the scar is still there! Dad apologized, but it wasn't really his fault; he didn't know anything about the game!

From infancy to about the age of six, I suffered from bronchial asthma. At eight months of age, I had been to the hospital and been put in an oxygen tent to help my breathing, and as I grew up, I used to take Ventolin from time to time when I was having trouble.

In the 1970s, the only way to take Ventolin was in liquid form; you could not inhale it through an inhaler as people do now. My mum and dad used to keep all the medicine in a tall, green cabinet on the top shelf, well out of my reach.

I have always had a bit of a sweet tooth, and in the 1970s, they filled medicines with sugar, so kids would find them easier to swallow. So, not only did Ventolin help me breathe, but it tasted pretty good, and I liked it.

One afternoon when my parents had gone out and our cousins were looking after us, I was feeling like something sweet. So, I decided to climb the shelves in the green cabinet and have a sip of my medicine. I knew it was good for me, and it tasted good, so I climbed up the shelves, grabbed the bottle, and climbed back down again.

I got the lid off the bottle – nothing is really childproof – and had a sip. It was pretty good, so I had another and another. Before I knew it, the bottle was empty. So, I put it in the bin and headed out into the lounge room to play.

About fifteen minutes later, my parents walked in the front door. "Hi, we're home," said Mum. "Hope you had fun while we were out."

"I did," I said, "I drank my whole bottle of medicine."

Mum and Dad looked at each other in shock. "Where's the bottle?" asked Dad.

"In the bin," I replied.

"You get the bottle," he said to Mum, "and I will put him in the car. We are going straight to the hospital."

I didn't really understand what all the fuss was about. All I did was drink my own medicine, but it seemed like I was in big trouble!

"What's wrong?" I asked Mum. "Why are we going to the hospital?"

Mum didn't say anything, but Dad spoke for her. "We are just a bit worried that maybe you had too much of your medicine, so we are going to take you to the doctor to check and make sure you didn't have too much," he said.

Dad was driving the car pretty fast, much faster than he normally did. Sitting in the back seat, I began to feel a bit strange. My tummy was doing flip-flops, and I felt a bit hot. There were no seat belts in the back, so I just held on to Mum tight and closed my eyes.

Dad dropped Mum and me off at the door to the hospital, and then he drove off to park the car. Mum carried me into the hospital, and I blacked out. The next thing I remember is lying in a bed with a tube down my throat and people all around me talking. Someone told me they were trying to get the medicine out of my stomach. I remember waking up a couple more times in that same bed. I couldn't swallow because of the tube down my throat, but I blacked out again pretty quickly each time.

The next thing I remember is waking up in a bed in my pyjamas. It was dark and quiet, and my parents weren't there. My hand hurt, and when I looked down at it, I saw a needle sticking out of it, sticky taped to hold it in. It was connected to a long tube that went up to a plastic bag hanging on a hook next to the bed. After what was probably only a few minutes, a nurse came over to my bed to talk to me.

"How are you feeling?" she said. I was too scared to reply. She patted me gently on the forehead. "Are you okay?" she asked. I nodded. My throat hurt, and I felt completely alone, but I was too scared to say a word to this lady I didn't know. "If you need anything, just call me, and I will come over and help you. If you need to use the potty, please let me know. I don't want to have to change the sheets on your bed." And then she was gone.

I lay there frozen in silence. I hadn't needed to go to the toilet before she mentioned it, but since that moment, I desperately needed to go. But I was so scared that I said nothing, and I rolled over and tried to go back to sleep.

The next time I woke up, I was saturated and freezing cold. The nurse was back. She pulled the covers off my bed, and another person in a blue shirt lifted me out of the bed and carried me to the bathroom, where they changed my clothes. When I got back, the bed was dry, and the nurse explained again that if I needed to go to the toilet to please call her, and she would help me.

The next time I woke up, I needed to go to the toilet again. I was still very scared, but I also didn't want to get into trouble, so I called out very quietly, "Nurse, Nurse." I waited a minute or two and basically just whispered "Nurse, Nurse." But no one came. This was my way of being obedient and doing what I was told; it was the right thing to do! But I did it in such a way that no one would notice me. I made it through the night and was much happier the next day when Mum and Dad arrived back at the hospital, although I did annoy the nurse who had to change the sheets on my bed a couple more times before the night was over.

I found out when I was much older that I nearly died three times during the night because Ventolin increases your adrenaline and causes a high heart rate, so it was pretty serious. The hospital was a scary place for me for many years. Whenever I walked into a hospital, I would feel faint and woozy. Just the smell of a hospital would have me feeling sick in my stomach. I don't know what the chemical was they used to keep hospitals clean back then, but it smelled like a swimming pool with way too much chlorine in it. In some rooms, the smell was stronger than others, and it would sit with you even after you left and were heading home in the car. It was like it stuck to you till you changed your clothes.

The worst part was that even though I was going through something so frightening, my parents were not allowed to stay the night at the hospital with me because back then, there were strict rules about parents having to go home. It must have been very hard for them too, to have to go home and not know if I was going to make it through the night!

2

Stepping Out

My father's job kept us moving around the country, and in 1978, we moved to Melbourne, to the suburb of Doncaster. Doncaster was a busy and growing suburb with a big shopping centre, big churches, and big schools. Everything felt bigger than what I was used to.

My parents enrolled me in the local primary school, a big school with several hundred students. I was a quiet kid, and it was a bit of a challenge for me to make friends. But I could already read before I started school, and I learned fast. My classroom had about twenty students, and my teacher's name was Mrs. Smith.

In my class, there was another boy called Josiah. While we had the same name, we had quite different personalities. While I was quiet and kept to myself, Josiah was outgoing and loud. He talked a great deal in class and seemed to get noticed a lot more than me. That was fine with me; I preferred not to get noticed too much. What I didn't know at the time, though, was how much my experiences with Josiah in my class would shape my view of school for several years to come.

For my fourth birthday, just before I started school, my mum and dad got me a bright-green bug catcher. I had been asking and asking them for it for weeks, so when my birthday came along and I opened it up, I was very excited.

It was shaped like a large bottle, but the top was sealed, and the lid was a green plastic base on the bottom. The idea was you put the base down on the ground near a bug, and when the bug crawled onto the base, you put the bottle-shaped bit over the top to trap the bug. It had holes in the top for air, and you could keep the bug there for a while and feed it through the top by taking off the lid.

The bug catcher was my favourite new toy. My dad taught me how to use it, and before he knew it, I was running around outside, trying to catch bugs, flies, lizards, or anything else I could find. I was mighty proud of it and decided to take my bug catcher to show-and-tell at school.

On the day of show-and-tell, I was pretty excited. I got to school, went into the classroom, put the bug catcher on the table at the front of the classroom so the class could see it, and went to sit at my desk. While I was waiting to be called up to the front for show-and-tell, Josiah came through the classroom door and saw my bug catcher on the front desk. He swung his arm at the bug catcher and sent it flying across the room, smashing into pieces on the wall. I was shocked. I couldn't imagine why anyone would want to randomly smash someone else's belongings. I just sat there stunned while Josiah laughed out loud and headed towards his desk.

Mrs. Smith stood up from her desk and called Josiah back to the front of the class. She sent Josiah to the principal's office, and she told me that he would have to buy me a replacement bug catcher that was brand new. From that day onwards, the teacher called me the good Josiah and called him the bad Josiah. Later on, I felt sorry for the other Josiah; being called the bad Josiah would not have been fun. These days, you would never get away with it, but Mrs. Smith did it for the rest of that year.

From that day onwards, bad Josiah did whatever he could think of to make sure I knew he hated me, and he tried to get other kids in the class to hate me too. For the rest of that year, I hated going to school.

To be honest, I started to feel quite lonely and isolated outside of home. Withdrawing from others was one of the ways I decided I could keep myself safe. I would go to my room and read books and spent a lot of time on my own. A lot of thoughts went through my head, but I never really shared them.

It wasn't all bad, though. The school had its fortieth school anniversary, and I was chosen as the only prep student to plant a tree at the back of the oval to celebrate it. That was pretty cool, and if the school hadn't been demolished twenty years later, the tree might still be there.

My school was about a kilometre and a half away from where we lived, and even though five years old was pretty young, my parents let me walk home from school in the afternoons. It would take me fifteen to twenty minutes to get home, and for the first week or so, my mother walked me home so I would know how to get there. After that, I was on my own.

The school had a road out the front, and there was a T-intersection about halfway down where the road came in at ninety degrees. Once school was over, some kids would go right, some would go left, and some would go straight ahead toward the hill. I had to turn left to head home, and I always wondered where the kids who went straight up into the hills disappeared to. I wanted to know where that road led.

One afternoon, my curiosity got the better of me, and I decided it was the perfect day to see where all these other kids went. So, instead of turning left to head home, I went straight ahead up the road and over the hill.

I walked for a long time, and I began to worry that I might get in trouble for doing this. But the feeling passed, and I kept going. I turned left up another inter-esting street with some huge houses, and then turned right, but soon I began to realize that I had no idea where I was.

I decided I had better do something about it, so I chose a house on the left-hand side of the street and pushed the front gate open. It was a single-floor house that was made of big cement bricks on corners of the house and had smaller red bricks in the walls. I walked up to the door and rang the bell. A lady answered the door. She was wearing a white dress with hundreds of small red roses on it and had thick spectacles on.

"Oh, hello there. What brings you here?" she asked.

"I got lost on my way home. I need to call my mum so she can come to get me. I was supposed to be home a long time ago, but I don't remember the way," I told her.

"What is your name?" she asked me.

"Josiah," I answered.

"My name is Jenny," she said, and she invited me in the door and called my mum for me.

Jenny spoke to my mum for a bit and then handed me the phone. "Hi, Mum," I said.

"Josiah, are you okay?" she said in a pretty wobbly voice.

"I'm fine, Mum. I walked up the hill near school to see where the other kids go, but I got lost," I said.

Mum was quiet for a bit and then said, "Well, we can talk about that when you get home. Can you give the phone back to Jenny?"

"Ok, Mum," I said, and I handed the phone to Jenny.

Once Jenny put the phone down, she told me that my dad would be coming to get me, so I sat down in her living room to wait. When my dad arrived, I was pretty glad to see him, but he was very quiet. He said thank you to Jenny, and we got into the car to head home. Dad didn't say a word for a while, and then he spoke.

"You really worried your mum and me. What were you thinking?"

"I wanted to see where the other kids went," I replied.

"Why would you do that?" he asked.

"I wanted to find out," I said.

"Well, don't do that again," he replied. "We didn't know where you were. You could have been anywhere. Someone could have picked you up and taken you away."

I didn't know what to say to that, and Dad remained silent the rest of the way home.

When I arrived home, Mum gave me a big hug. When she let me go, she said, "What made you think to knock on someone's door?"

I replied, "I was lost, and I thought that was the only way I could get someone to help me." Mum smiled and told me that was a good idea and then sent me off to play in the lounge room. Neither Mum nor Dad really said anything much more about it. In fact, I wasn't even really punished at all. I think Mum and Dad were just so grateful that I was all right.

I often made decisions that made perfect sense to me but didn't seem to make quite as much sense to everyone else. I have always kept my thoughts to myself, which made it harder for other people to understand what I was thinking. They didn't know what I didn't tell them.

I discovered that the best way to learn was by doing things. While I loved reading stories and making them up as well, I learnt best by trying things out, making mistakes, and having another go at it.

3

On the Move

In 1979, my family and I moved from Melbourne to a small town called Loxton in South Australia. Loxton is on the edge of Murray River and is part of the Riverland area, which includes several similar smallish towns. The Riverland is a citrus-growing area and becomes extremely hot in the summer. It was common in January and February to have a few weeks where it was over forty degrees Celsius during the day and around thirty degrees Celsius at night. Winters could be cold but were often dry. I hardly remember wearing a raincoat in the whole four years I lived there.

In the late seventies, about 6,500 people lived in Loxton, so it was a small but vibrant town. At one end of the main street are the river and the Historical Village, a museum with buildings, farm tools, and other items from the eighteenth and nineteenth centuries. At the other end of the main street is a large roundabout where the three main roads of the town joined together with the main street. Just past the big roundabout was my father's office in the Department of Agriculture.

Our new house was a small three-bedroom home with a fireplace in the lounge room, timber floors, and a red concrete veranda out the front. After moving in, my parents looked for a local church to attend, and we found one that was walking distance from our new house. The main street and most of the town was walking distance from our new home. Mum and Dad also enrolled my brother, Matt, and me into the local government primary school.

My first week at school was a bit messed up. I was beginning school a couple of days late in first term, so when I was brought along to my first class, the students and teacher had already had a couple of days to get to know each other. One of the office ladies took me to my new class, walked me through the door, and introduced me to Mr. Wallace, and Mr. Wallace introduced me to the class.

"This is Josiah, a new student to our school. Please make him welcome and help him settle into our school," he said to the class. "There is a spare seat on the table at the back," he said and pointed to a seat at a table with three other boys towards the back of the room. So, I headed over put my school bag on the floor next to my feet and sat down.

That first day was very confusing. I could not make any sense of what I was being taught. But when confronted with a problem, I usually did one of two things, try to solve it or try to ignore it. In this case, I tried my best to solve it by concentrating and working as hard as I could. But no matter how hard I tried, the work was very difficult.

The next couple of weeks of school were hard work. Most of the time, I had no idea what Mr. Wallace was talking about, and I tried so hard to learn it all, sometimes I lost track of what was happening around me.

On the Friday of my second week at school, we had maths for our first lesson of the day. We were all sitting at our desks trying to complete a worksheet of maths questions we had been given. I was pretty focused on trying to make sense of these questions, so I was really concentrating on the work in front of me.

Suddenly, I realised that I couldn't hear anyone talking. I couldn't hear any pens writing on paper. It was very quiet. I looked up, and the other boys were no longer sitting at the desk with me. I turned my head around to look at the rest of the classroom, and I realised I was all alone. I stood up to see what was going on, and I heard a huge burst of laughter from the corner of the room.

Mr. Wallace and the rest of the students were sitting on the mat, waiting for me to notice them. I had been so off in my own world trying to do this impossible maths work that I hadn't even noticed Mr. Wallace and the whole class move to the mat without me!

"Calm down, class," said Mr. Wallace. "C'mon, Josiah, come over here and join the rest of us."

I felt so embarrassed and tried to make myself shrink into the floor as I headed over to the mat. I couldn't believe I could be so stupid not to notice everyone leaving their desks. They thought that it was a great joke, but I felt small and silly.

Just before lunch, one of the ladies from the office came into the class to speak to Mr. Wallace. Then she came to speak to me.

"Josiah, it seems that when you were enrolled in our school, we put you in the wrong class. This is grade two, and you are supposed to be in grade one, so pack up your things, and I will take you to your new class."

I felt relieved, at least I wouldn't have to deal with the embarrassment I felt anymore. I didn't really have any idea what the office lady was talking about or why I had been in the wrong class. My parents explained to me later that it was the result of having moved from Victoria to South Australia. The school had thought I was further ahead than I was and got their enrolment of me wrong. I was happy to see the back of Mr. Wallace. I didn't really like him much, and my new teacher seemed a lot kinder.

I was an incredibly curious kid. I would ask anyone a question about pretty much anything. But I also liked to try things out too. In fact, I often tried things out without thinking them through first. One Sunday afternoon, Dad was driving Matt and me and some other kids from church out to one of the fruit blocks on the outside of town. While we were driving, a thought went through my head. *I wonder what it would be like to be driving along in a car with the door open so I could see the road as it went flying past.* So, before I had thought about it for one more second, I had opened the car door and was looking down at the road surface right in front of my nose.

This freaked out pretty much everyone else in the car. My dad yelled at me, "*Shut the door* and don't ever do that again! What were you thinking? Use your head. You could have fallen out!" The other kids got a bit of a fright, but I thought Dad was being a bit dramatic. No one was hurt, and I really just wanted to see the road go by super-fast up close! Although having no seat belts in the back of the car certainly made opening the door a bit risky.

As a kid growing up, I was quite happy being on my own. I didn't need a big group of friends. Usually, I would find one friend, and that would be all I needed. Arriving in Loxton, I had never changed schools before, and it took me quite a while to make friends. At Loxton Primary, that one friend was a girl in my class called Louise. Louise was the coolest kid I knew. Louise lived across the road from the school, and her parents ran a removalist and second-hand furniture business. Her parents were pretty strict, but because her parents knew my parents, they let us hang out.

Next to Louise's house was a vacant block where

we used to hit a golf ball around and build our underground cubby house. Well, when I say *underground
cubby house*, I mean a big hole we dug in the ground and
then covered over with a couple of large pieces of tin.
We didn't know much about building things, so it was
pretty basic. In summer, the tin roof made the cubby
house extremely hot.

One Saturday afternoon, we were hanging out in
our cubby house talking, and I heard a noise on the roof.

"Did you hear a noise?" I asked Louise.

"Yeah," she said, "I wonder what it was. Why
don't you have a look and see what it is?"

So, I cautiously lifted up one side of the tin roof
from the middle of the cubby house and stuck my head
through the gap to have a look. At first, I couldn't see
anything because it was so bright. There was nothing to
see at first, so I swivelled my head around to look behind
me, and I froze on the spot. Looking back at me was a big
black snake, bigger than I had ever seen in my life, and it
was staring right at me!

I could not move a muscle, Louise tapped my arm
and said "What is it? What is it?"

But I couldn't speak; the snake was right in front
of me! I began to slowly lower my head back inside the
cubby house. So slowly it felt like ages before my head
was back under the roof and I could breathe again!

When I had put the roof down, Louise asked me
again, "What is it?"

Trying to sound calm, I replied, "It's a snake, a huge black snake!"

Louise started to go pale. The snake looked to me like a red-bellied black snake, which I knew was quite poisonous.

So, we were stuck, it was boiling hot, and a big poisonous snake was sitting on the tin roof of our hole in the ground.

I said to Louise, "It looks like we are stuck here. That snake is not going anywhere. But we don't want to scare it. What if it comes through the hole in the tin and joins us!"

We were both terrified and sat together holding hands, huddled in the corner, waiting for the snake to move on. But it was quite happy sunning itself on our tin roof for what felt like ages.

Louise is the first real friend I remember having as a child who seemed to like me just for being me. I didn't have to pretend to be anyone else. So, despite being frightened, it felt good to be in this situation with a true friend.

After we had sat there for a while, it was getting pretty hot. I said to Louise "We have to do something. We can't just sit here all day."

"What can we do?" she said.

"I have no idea."

We both thought about it for a while, and then

Louise had an idea. "If we both moved over to one side of the cubby house and crouched under the tin roof, where the snake is, we could jump up and flip the tin over with the snake on the ground and make a run for it."

I was sceptical at first. "What if the tin flips up and the snake falls in here with us?" I asked.

"It won't," she said. "We can do this!"

I couldn't think of a better plan, so we moved over to the side of our cubby house where the snake was sunning itself on our roof. We both got ourselves into position, crouched under the piece of tin the snake was on, up on our feet, and then we counted down, three, two, one, and we both launched ourselves into the piece of tin, head and shoulders first. The tin tipped up and over away from our hole in the ground and flipped over. We both jumped out of the cubby house and ran like hell to get out of there. We had no idea what happened to the snake, and we weren't waiting around to find out! We didn't stop running till we got back inside Louise's house, arriving in the kitchen with a huge rush.

"What's chasing you?" said Louise's mum.

"A huge black snake!" I replied.

"What on earth is going on?" she asked.

So, we told her the story, and she gave Louise a big hug and told us she was glad we were okay, and that I had better head on home because it was getting late. As I headed home, thinking about what had happened, I realised just how dangerous a situation we were in, and my hands began to shake. I felt so faint I had to stop walking and rest for a while. I did learn something that day, though: a scary experience is nowhere near as scary when you're in it with a great friend.

4

Barry the Bully

At school in grade four, I confronted my first serious bully. His name was Barry, and he was the only kid in our year group who was taller than me. He was aggressive, and he seemed angry all the time; he used to push kids around in the line while we were waiting to go into class. On the playground, he would insist on controlling what games were played, how they were played, and what the rules were. If anyone disagreed, he would push them over or punch them.

Experiencing this for myself and watching others getting more and more frustrated with the way Barry was treating them, I decided to ask Dad about it.

"Dad, there is a kid at school who keeps pushing other kids around, trying to tell everyone what to do, and if anyone disagrees with him, he flattens them," I said. "The teachers don't seem to do anything about it, even when it seems obvious to us what he's doing. What can I do about it?"

"Dealing with bullies can be difficult," said Dad. "When I was bullied at school, I would find the biggest, strongest kid in my year group and make friends with them. That way I was always protected,"

How am I supposed to do that? I thought to myself. Dad's answer made sense to him, but I had no idea how to make Barry into a friend.

"How did you do that, Dad?"

"Find something in common. Is he a football fan, is he into cars, what's the thing he loves to do? Figure that out, learn about it, and then bring it up in conversation and see what happens."

So, I decided to try dad's idea.

I put my plan into action and tried becoming friends with Barry. He was a pretty rough kid. He played Australian Rules football and finally ended up playing professionally. Barry's mum wasn't around; it was just him and his dad. His house was on my way home, so I started trying to talk with Barry and walk home with him after school. On the way home, there was another house we walked past, which was being constructed. They had put in the windows, and the frame was up, but the walls and roof were still being constructed. One day, while I was walking home with Barry, he picked up a few stones and threw them at the windows, breaking the glass. There were no workers around, so he broke another one. I decided to join in, and I picked up a decent-size rock and broke a window as well. The next day, when we were walking past the house, the glass had been replaced, so we both threw rocks through the windows and broke them again, and then ran like crazy.

That's pretty much how I learned to be friends with Barry. If I did or was prepared to do what he was doing, then he would be my friend.

I did find out much later that Dad had left out one vital piece of information from his own experiences. He had done the bully's homework to make sure he never got bullied! But breaking windows seemed to work for me.

Another time, I was walking home with Barry, and he told me he had something he wanted to show me. Hidden in his backyard under a hole in the fence, he had three magazines full of pictures of naked women. Barry told me he had stolen them from his dad. I had never seen anything like it before; I was only nine years old, after all.

I headed home, and when I got there, I told my dad all about it. I never told him about breaking the windows; I knew that was wrong. But I had never seen anything like this before. I was so surprised by the whole thing, I just blurted out the story. I even told him where they were hidden.

Dad was pretty shocked at my story. Like most parents, I think he saw himself as being able to protect his children from the bad things in the world. But unfortunately, parents really have much less control over this than we would like to think.

Dad told me to show him where the magazines were, so I took him with me. We went to Barry's house and into the shed. I showed him where they were. He took them out and then confronted Barry's father with it. That was the point when my relationship with Barry became very stressed. We were both so young. He didn't understand why I would go and tell my dad. I didn't understand why that was a big deal. I had just told my dad; what was so wrong with that?

My strategy to make friends with Barry wasn't turning out to be very easy. I was getting into trouble myself, and I didn't feel much safer at school than I had before.

The next day, Barry was super cranky with me and didn't speak to me at school that whole day. After school, I tried to walk home with him, but he pretty much ignored me the whole way. As we walked down the main street, we went past a fairly big shop. It was a farmer-owned store called Eudunda Supermarkets. There were a number of them around South Australia, selling all kinds of things. This particular store was like an old-school Woolworth's or Costco. They sold everything from food to toys to decorations and snacks.

Barry finally spoke. "Let's go in here. I want to get a Rubik's Cube."

"Sure, but I didn't bring any money with me to buy anything."

"Me either," replied Barry. "It doesn't matter. I steal from here all the time. It's easy! You can too."

I felt a sudden shot of adrenaline. Stealing was something I had never considered before. I knew it was wrong, but I was in a dilemma. I needed to be friends with Barry for my own protection, but what if we got caught?

I followed Barry into the shop while desperately trying to decide what to do. That's when I realized that my little brother was with us as well; Matt was following us home, and now he was following us through the store, and I had kind of forgotten he was there. This was trouble! Even if I stole something and didn't get caught in the store, my brother would know about it and might tell our parents.

We all headed towards the toy section. I said to Barry, "Are you really going to steal a Rubik Cube?"

"Shut up!" he whispered. "Someone will hear you!"

Matt was following along and heard what I said. He asked, "What are you doing, Josiah? If you steal something, you are going to get into trouble."

"Not if you do it too!" I replied. I figured if I was going to be friends with Barry and steal something with him, the best way to make sure Matt didn't tell anyone was to get him to take something as well. Then he wouldn't be able to tell on me.

"C'mon, Matt," I said, "it will be okay. Barry says

it's easy."

"Nope, I won't do it," said Matt. "It's not right, and you will get into huge trouble with Dad if you get caught."

"All right, well, it's your loss," and we all headed to the toy section of the store. I was worried that Matt would dob when we got home, but I was determined to prove to Barry I could do anything he did.

When we arrived in the toy section, we looked through the toys. Barry found the Rubik's Cube he wanted and stashed it in his school bag. I picked up a couple of cool Christmas decorations and hid them in my bag. We never had fancy ones at home, and these would look cool on the Christmas tree. It might seem like an unusual thing to steal, but they were items I could never have bought for myself.

As soon as we finished putting them in our school bags, a staff person in a uniform walked around the corner.

"What have you got in your school bags?" he said sternly. "I overheard you planning to steal some toys. Let me see what's in your bags right now!"

The three of us looked at each other. We had been caught red-handed! None of us said a word. We didn't open our bags. We just stood there and looked at the guy and waited to see what would happen next.

"I think you better come with me," he said. "We will see what the manager wants to do."

We were too scared to run! So, we followed him to the manager's office. The manager was an old guy called Steve, or at least that's what his nametag said. He had grey hair and a big moustache and was wearing a brown suit with a wide brown tie.

We walked into the office, and the guy who caught us told Manager Steve what he had seen and heard, and then he left with the three of us sitting on the floor, holding our school bags.

Steve stood up from behind his desk, leaned forward, and spoke. "Boys, we know you stole something. You certainly look pretty guilty. I want you to open up your bags so I can see what you took."

Matt opened his bag, and Manager Steve looked inside it. "Nothin' in here," he said. "Right," and he pointed to me. "You next. What you got in there?"

I opened my bag, and the two Christmas decorations were sitting there on the top of my schoolbooks for all to see.

"Give them to me," he said, and I meekly handed them over. Then it was Barry's turn. Well, Barry had obviously been in this kind of situation before. He looked angry rather than scared.

"Open your bag," Manager Steve said to Barry.

"No way," said Barry, "and you can't make me."

"You had better open that bag" said Manager Steve, "or I will call the police!"

Barry didn't budge; he just stared back defiantly at Manager Steve. So, the manager picked up the phone off his desk and called the police. At least that's what we assumed he did. His phone had a long cord on it, so he walked out of his office to talk on the phone, and we couldn't hear what he was saying.

I don't know why we didn't just run out the door. It's not like he could have grabbed us or tied us up or anything, but we were pretty much just frozen in place on our backsides on the floor. We just sat there and waited till Steve came back through the door and put his phone down on the desk.

"I have spoken to the police," he said. "They are on their way to talk to you, and they will be informing your parents of what has happened here today. So, sit there and wait."

Then he turned his back on us, walked out of the office, and closed the door. None of us spoke to each other. Matt looked like he was about to cry. Barry still looked very angry, and I just felt nervous and scared. I had that horrible feeling in the pit of my stomach again that told me something bad was coming.

I think that was the worst part, sitting there waiting for the police to arrive. The office window looked out over the car park, so we saw the police car arrive. The two policemen got out of their car and walked into the store. They stopped outside the office while Manager Steve explained what he knew. Then the door opened, and the two policemen walked in and stood just inside the doorway.

"Okay, let's see what you boys have in your bags," said the taller one with the moustache. He walked over to Barry's bag and picked it up and had a look inside, immediately finding the Rubik's Cube.

"Okay, we'd better have your names and addresses," said the other policeman. "We will be driving you home to your parents to talk to them about what you have done here."

So, we all gave the policeman our names and addresses. Barry tried to lie, but the policeman already knew who he was.

Then he turned to Manager Steve and said, "Anything you want to say to these boys before we take them to talk with their parents?"

The manager leaned over us and said, "I am very disappointed in you boys. Unfortunately, you will no longer be allowed into this store without a parent or another adult to supervise you. I can't have boys who steal in my store."

The policeman with the moustache picked up the stolen items and gave them to the manager and then motioned for us to follow him out the door to the police car. So, we picked up our schoolbags and followed them out the door and sat in the back of the police car together.

I knew that when they talked to my dad, all hell was

going to break loose. My father was a good dad, but he was strict, and when he got angry, he gave big punishments. I knew I would be losing my favourite toy or something else of value for a long time. Nevertheless, I had nowhere else to go, so I stepped into the back of the police car with Barry and Matt, and off we went.

They dropped off Barry first, and all that did was give me time to worry about how much trouble I would be in. Luckily, when we got home, Dad wasn't there. The police talked to my mum and told her everything. I was somewhat happy. I thought that this meant I wouldn't get into so much trouble after all. The police left, and Mum told me to go to my room and wait for my dad to arrive.

After a few hours, Dad finally came home. He came straight into my room to talk to me. His reaction was not what I was expecting. I was expecting him to be angry, but he wasn't.

"Josiah" he said, "I never thought that this was one of the things I would need to deal with. I just didn't think you would do something like this. I am just so disappointed."

The more he talked, the sadder he got. I didn't know what to do or say because I couldn't remember ever seeing him like this before. It never occurred to me that the things I did would have any effect on my dad. That by doing the wrong thing, I would be causing him pain.

It was an important lesson for me to learn, that what I

did had an impact on the people around me, and sometimes not for the better. In the end I didn't get any kind
of punishment at all from Mum and Dad; mind you,
the experience of begin told off by the police was scary
enough.

5

It's Easier Not to be Great

We lived in Loxton for four years, and at the end of grade four, our family moved to Melbourne. Melbourne in the early 1980s was very different from Loxton. It was a big, busy city with hundreds of thousands of people. Even the suburb we moved to, Blackburn, was almost ten times the size of Loxton. So many cars and traffic and such a different way of living.

Moving to Melbourne meant big changes. I had never lived in a city before. The environment was different; there were no open spaces and spacious horizons. Everything felt closed in and busy, and there were people everywhere. The people were different too. In Loxton, when you walked along the street, people would say hello to each other and sometimes stop for a chat with someone they knew. In Melbourne, you could walk from one place to another without anyone ever saying hello or even seeing someone you knew.

When we moved to Melbourne, our parents enrolled my younger brother Matt and me into Blackburn Primary School. It was an old school but a good school, although a traditional one. Everything about the school looked and felt old. Take the desks; all the classrooms had old-school desks that were arranged in rows facing the front of the class. Children would sit in five or six rows in the classroom. The desks were so old, they actually had inkwell holes at the front of the desk where you could keep your inkpots in the olden days. This was so that you could dip your pen or quill into it while writing. Two students sat at each desk. The chairs were built into the desks, so you couldn't move them at all. The school was built around 1885, so by the time I came there in 1993, it was more than a hundred years old.

That first day at a new school was always pretty scary for me. I liked certainty. I felt comfortable in places I knew well and terribly uncomfortable in places that were new. On our first day, Mum took Matt and me to school. We met our new teachers during recess on that first day, and then we followed our teachers to class to meet all the other students in our class.

My teacher was a tall, skinny man who wore glasses and looked very intelligent. He began by introducing me to the class.

"Good morning, class. Josiah is a new student in our school. He and his family have moved to Melbourne from interstate, and I am sure you will all make him welcome."

The other students gave me a quick clap, and then the teacher said, "Josiah, there is a spare desk in the third row next to Greg. Why don't you go and sit there and get settled in, and I am sure Greg can show you around the school for the day. Is that all right, Greg?"

"Sure," replied Greg, so I went and sat down, opened my school bag, and put my books and materials away in my desk. The desks had a lift-up lid with a big space underneath for all your textbooks and workbooks, pens and pencils. Even my calculator fit in there with room to spare.

Our first subject for the day was maths. Our teacher, whose name I couldn't remember or pronounce, started to write the questions we had to answer up on the blackboard. Our job was to write the question into our workbook, work out the answer, and then go on to the next one. So, I dutifully copied the work from the blackboard into my workbook and made attempt at answering the questions. However, I had never seen maths like this before. The maths questions had letters in them. I thought maths was all about the numbers. Since when did letters come into maths? I felt like the dumbest kid in the class, but I kept this to myself rather than asking for help, as I didn't want to stand out on my first day.

After working away at this for most of the lesson, there was a knock at the door, and the deputy principal came into the class and spoke to the teacher. Then she came over to me.

"I am so sorry," she said. "You were supposed to be put into the grade-five class, but the ladies in the office made a mistake, and this is grade six." So, pack your books back into your bag, and I will take you to the correct class."

Not again! I thought to myself. No wonder I couldn't make any sense of this maths work. I don't know how the mistake was made this time, I guess it was because I had finished grade four in South Australia, and the system there was different from Victoria, and they mucked it up again. So, I packed my bag and followed the deputy principal out the door off to meet a new group of strangers.

Sometimes in life, you meet someone who makes you feel special. Someone who helps you understand your true value. I didn't know it, but when I walked into that grade five class, I was going to meet exactly that kind of person. At that moment in time, though, I was frustrated, which was really a cover for my anxiousness. I had to be reintroduced to a new class, meet a new teacher, find a new desk, and begin work all over again.

The deputy principal opened the door and motioned for me to go into the classroom in front of her. All the students stopped working and looked straight at me, not something I enjoyed. I walked through the door, and the deputy principal introduced me.

44

"Mrs. McGinn, year five, this is Josiah. He will be in your class this year. He has moved with his family to Melbourne, and I hope you will make him welcome."

Then she shut the door behind me, and I was left standing there just inside the door with the whole class just staring, or at least that's what it felt like to me. I looked nervously up at my new teacher, and I was greeted with a wonderful, gentle smile.

"Hi, Josiah," she said. "Welcome to grade five. We are so glad you're here. Class, this is Josiah. Please make him welcome and show him around the school during recess. In the meantime, Josiah, how about you sit at this desk next to Michelle and unpack your books while we get back to our lesson."

So, I carried my school bag over to the third-row desk where Michelle was seated and sat down. I began unpacking all over again, lifting the lid on the desk and emptying all my books inside.

Mrs. McGinn became my favourite schoolteacher of all time. She was kind and friendly, and she had this way of meeting your gaze that made you feel like you had her full attention. She was full of encouragement too and loved listening to our stories. For a while, I actually began to look forward to going to school!

My younger brother, Matt, wasn't so lucky. He was in grade four, and his teacher was the exact opposite of Mrs. McGinn. She was very tough, very strict, and totally unpredictable. She would get angry with the students, lose her temper, and hand out unreasonable consequences. During maths class, about four weeks into the school year, one of the boys in Matt's class was talking too loudly. So, Matt's teacher just picked him up and locked him up in the cupboard in the corner of the classroom. The news got around, and parents made some complaints to the school. A few weeks later, she was transferred out of the school to an office job because of her poor behaviour.

Now, this was good news and bad news. The good news was that Matt's class was free of their teacher and her unpredictable anger. The bad news (well, not all bad) was that the school didn't have a replacement teacher, so they decided to merge several classes together. My grade five class became a grade four and five composite class, and some of the grade four students, including Matt, joined us.

Matt and I are close in age, and at times that led to quite a few arguments and fights with each other. So, I wasn't that excited about Matt and me sharing a class together. The class was going to be bigger than it was before, and Matt and I would be in the same space 24/7! I think he was even less excited than I was.

However, this period of enjoying school didn't last, and it had nothing to do with having Matt in my class. It wasn't very long before I was being confronted by a bully again, and as a result, I made a decision that would have a long-term impact on my life.

One of the ways Mrs. McGinn used to help us

learn was through competition. It was something that inspired us boys especially with our learning. One of the ways she did this was to create a maths competition. Our class had six rows of desks all facing the front. She would ask two students to stand level with the back row of desks and then ask them a maths question. The student who answered it correctly would move forward one row until they reached the front of the classroom. This meant getting seven answers right to win.

At the end of each week, there was a challenge for class champion. A new student would go up against the previous week's winner. Jeremy was very good at maths. He won the first seven weeks of term in a row. Jeremy was a big kid. Not that I was small. I was usually the tallest or second-tallest kid in my class, but Jeremy had me beat. He was not only taller but also bigger than me.

In the eighth week of that first term, I had a good week and was chosen by Mrs. McGinn to challenge Jeremy for class champion. I was keen to do my best, so I was concentrating hard as the competition began. The competition was very close. Jeremy would get an answer right, and then I would get an answer right and draw level with him. In the end, we were on the fourth row, and Jeremy answered two consecutive questions and went to the sixth row. Now all he had to do was to answer one more question and once again become the undefeated class champion.

The next two questions were tough. The first was a long division question, which I worked out in my head and got right. The next question involved multiplying two numbers together and then taking another number away from the answer to get the result. To my surprise, Jeremy answered first and got the answer wrong! So, I had a free shot at getting the answer right. I worked it out in my head and answered the question. I got it right, and we drew level on the last desk together.

The next question Mrs. McGinn asked was a tough one, even for us. It had three steps to the solution. We both started working on it, but I was a little bit faster and gave the correct answer, forty-two. It felt pretty good to win, but if I had known what was coming next, I wouldn't have been as happy.

I went home and told my parents all about it. I injected plenty of suspense into the story about my historic comeback from two answers behind to win, which had them on the edge of their seats. On Monday morning, as I walked to school with Matt, I was still feeling pretty good. As we got to school, Matt ran off to play with his friends, and I started walking to our classroom. I saw Jeremy coming towards me with two of his friends.

Jeremy walked right up to me and pushed me in the chest, knocking me to the ground. To say that I was shocked would be an understatement. Jeremy stood over me, looking down at me. "Don't ever do that again" he said. "Nobody beats me in front of the class like that! If you beat me again, I am going to hurt you! Then he just stepped over me and walked away.

I felt sick in the stomach as I got up off the ground

and picked up my schoolbag. I stood there and watched as Jeremy and his mates walked away laughing, and a feeling of shame and fear welled over me. I made a decision; I was never going to stand out in the crowd again. Every single time I made an effort, did well in school, achieved something and felt good about it, I put a target on my back. The only way to avoid the bullies was not to be noticed.

Matt and I did compete against each other once that year, and he beat me too, which he reminded me of for quite a while, and while I might have let him get a couple of the answers over me early, he beat me fair and square.

Fading into the shadows at a new school wasn't too difficult. At lunchtimes I went to the library to read books; during recess I sat quietly near the classroom and waited for it to be over. I gave up trying to get good grades and work hard. I didn't want to stand out in that area either. The more I played it safe, the better I felt.

So, the year kind of meandered along until a freezing-cold day in the middle of winter, when Sarah, one of the girls in our class, handed me a note during recess. The note said:

Hi Josiah,

I think you're pretty great, will you be my boyfriend?

Tammy xox

I didn't know Tammy well at all. But like me, she wasn't one of the popular kids, and her friend Sarah was even less popular. Other kids in our class would tease Sarah because they thought she was overweight. I didn't think about it much. I had no idea what she really meant by being her boyfriend; we had never really spoken much at all.

I nervously wrote *yes* on the note and gave it back to Sarah to pass on to Tammy. Nothing else happened for a few days except Tammy used to stare at me during class, which I did my best not to notice. We didn't even talk to each other let alone spend time together. I liked the idea of having a girlfriend, I made sure Matt knew all about it! But I had no idea how to talk to or act around someone who wanted to be my girlfriend; the idea of having a conversation with Tammy freaked me out.

After a few days I was in the library during lunchtime reading an Asterix and Obelix book, when Sarah came to find me and give me a new note from Tammy. The note simply read:

Do you like Sophie more than you like me?

Sarah just stood there waiting for a reply. I had no idea what to say. So, I just wrote *No* on the bottom of the note and gave it back to Sarah to give to Tammy. A few minutes later, Sarah returned to tell me that Tammy was very happy with my answer, and off she went.

I found this all very confusing. I had no idea what I was supposed to do or say. There was no way I was going to ask anyone about it either. That would be way too embarrassing!

After a few weeks of this kind of back-and-forth conversation, Tammy sent me a note with a message I didn't like at all. It said:

Hi Josiah,

I have decided that I don't want to have a boyfriend anymore, so I want to break up.

Sorry,

Tammy.

My social skills weren't great to begin with, but this was not something I was prepared for. While Tammy and I had never spoken a word to each other except through notes or messages, I felt quite sad and disappointed. The idea that I had a girlfriend was something I had found comforting, and it made me feel a bit important.

I couldn't think of anything to write back, so I told Sarah to tell Tammy I understood, and that was it. In my mind, I was back to being single and alone.

Later that year, it was announced that our class would be going on a camp to Wilson's Promontory. I was really looking forward to it. We were told that the birds there were so friendly that if you had some seed in your hand and stretched your arms out, Rosellas and other small birds would come and land on your arm and eat the birdseed while you stood there.

Unfortunately, with both Matt and me in the same class, my parents only had enough funds to send one of us to camp. So, they decided that neither one of us would go because it wouldn't be fair for one of us to go and the other to have to stay home. I thought that was unfair on me, as this was really my class, and without Matt having had such a terrible teacher, I would have been able to go. But once my parents had decided something like this, they were very hard to shift, and in the end, while I didn't like it, what they were saying made sense.

Matt and I spent the entire week of camp in the school library. There were no classes to go to, as everybody had left for camp. While I love reading, it was pretty dull sitting in one spot all day with nothing to do but read. The rest of the class were super excited about going away on a camp where birds would eat out of your hand. As a kid raised in the country, I would have loved that camp. Instead, I was stuck.

The kids from my class came back with a ton of stories to tell. It was one more thing that I wasn't a part of. The kids would have conversations about what happened at the camp, and I wouldn't get to be a part of it. Missing out on these kinds of experiences was something I had become used to.

Growing up, we didn't have TV at home, something I was convinced every other child had. There were a couple of reasons for this, and one of them was my own fault. When I was four years old, my dad had installed an aerial at our new house in Mount Gambier so he could tune into the TV channels. One afternoon, I leaned a ladder on the side of the house, and for a reason

I can't really remember, I got a pair of scissors and cut all the aerial wire into tiny pieces (I was probably thinking the same thing as when I opened the car door!) So, Dad put the TV in the cupboard, and after a few years, he threw it out, and we didn't get TV till I turned fourteen (which is another story for later).

Since I didn't have a TV in my house, it was another thing that made me feel different from other kids, like I didn't belong. Kids at school would continuously talk about what they were watching at home, and I'd have no idea what they were talking about. Teachers would sometimes give homework like *go and watch the news and write a report on it*. My parents would then send a note saying that we don't have a TV at home, so could you please give Josiah some other assignment? I felt like I didn't fit in anywhere.

6

Whitewater

At the end of that year, we moved again. Dad's job in Blackburn was finished, and he got a new job in Chadstone, one of Melbourne's poorer suburbs and at times a pretty rough place. Most of the houses around ours were provided by the government to people who couldn't afford to rent or buy a home of their own. There were lots of people living in very difficult situations. Single-parent families, people who couldn't find work, people who needed help and support, something my mum and dad are very good at.

Our house was next door to the church where my dad worked. It had a tiny backyard because the church had converted our backyard into a car park. So, while we had access to the church hall to play in, our backyard was so small, our trampoline took up almost half the space.

My school changed too. Matt and I were enrolled in Jordanville South Primary School. My parents didn't know it when they sent us there, but it was a really rough school. Most of the kids grew up in poor households with unhappy or uncertain home situations. Some of them had just one parent at home, and some had parents who were divorced. Some had parents who had remarried, and now the kids were living with stepparents. A lot of the parents were unemployed and finding it difficult to just to feed and clothe their kids. Australia was in the middle of a recession, and thousands of people had lost their jobs. Everyone was dealing with their own problems and hardships.

In the year before we started at Jordanville South Primary, a couple of teenage boys broke into the school library and set it on fire. The library was a standalone building at the end of a row of classrooms. The entire library was burned down to the ground, but the rest of the classrooms nearby were saved. By the time Matt and I arrived, the library was housed in a temporary building. It wasn't unusual in Chadstone in the mid-1980s for there to be vandalism and destruction of property like this.

It was all new to me, and my family and I were smack-bang in the middle of it all. We had just assumed that the community we lived in would be safe because we had always lived in safe places. But this was different.

In the beginning, I didn't think much about it, and off I went to school. It was my first day; I was in the sixth grade, and we were the oldest kids in the school, at the top of the pecking order for once. The school went from kindergarten all the way to the sixth grade. The families who lived around the school had all been there for most of their sons' and daughters' lives, so I was the only new kid in the whole of grade six. In fact, most of the other kids in grade six had been together since kindergarten. Many of the families who lived there aspired to move out of Chadstone, not into it.

The school had a very strong migrant community, with people from many different backgrounds. There were kids with Greek and Italian heritage, and others too. It was one of those suburbs where a lot of different races and groups of people lived together. The same was true for the school. Coming from the country, where most people belonged to the same ethnic group in those days, this was pretty new for me too. I had never spent any time in a multicultural place or school.

Some of the kids at the new school spoke other languages, which I found fascinating. Anything that they didn't want the teacher or any other student to hear, they would communicate in their own language. I wouldn't understand any of it, well, except for the swear words, which we all learnt pretty well.

A month into the school year, our teacher Mrs. West announced that the tryouts for the school cricket team were coming up soon. Now, I loved cricket. I loved watching it; I loved hearing about it on the radio. I loved it so much that when the first home test match started in November each year, I would fake an illness and stay at home so I could listen to the commentary on the radio all day long. It was one of my passions. I loved players like Allan Border, Dennis Lillee, and Rodney Marsh.

I always wanted to play cricket. At home, I would always play with my brother and father when he was around. I had even played cricket at his old primary school. So, obviously, I decided to try out for the school team. The grade five teacher, Mr Bowman, was the cricket coach; he would select all the players and choose the teams from grades five and six. The girls had their own team.

I went to the first team practice, and Mr. Bowman asked me what position I would like to play. I said I would be a good wicketkeeper. I had always wanted to play in that position, and I didn't like bowling anyway. I was also okay with batting further down the batting order. Well, Mr Bowman gave me some gloves and pads to put on and put me behind the stumps. Most of the players had come to bat, and a few of them had come to bowl, but I just wanted to be the wicketkeeper – fair and simple.

I stayed behind the stumps and made some tremendous catches, having a great time too. I felt like I did very well and that I could take up this position for the team permanently. Once the practice was over, Mr. Bowman told everyone that he would post a notice on the school board the next day. That's when everybody would find out who had made the team and who hadn't.

I felt very confident. A lot of the players were

in fierce competition with each other for batting and bowling positions, but there were only two of us who had tried out for the role of wicketkeeper. I felt like I had made some tremendous saves and taken some great catches and had even made two run-outs. So, the next day as I came to school, I went directly over to read the list of the team that had been finalized.

There was a group of boys, each from grade six and grade five in the team. Eleven players had been selected for the playing team, but the total team members were fifteen, so the team would have a few reserves. I read the notice and couldn't believe my eyes. Not only had I been made the wicketkeeper, but Mr. Bowman had also selected me to be the team captain. I was the wicketkeeper *and* the team captain, yes – talk about a bonus!

It was so unexpected, and I felt so honoured to have been selected by Mr. Bowman to lead the team. I had not tried out for the captain and wasn't expecting it either, so it was a bit of a shock, but in a good way. What I didn't realize was that there were some boys in the sixth grade who were not very happy about this turn of events. I had been in school for only a few weeks, and I was the new kid. I hadn't spent years in the school like they had, and they had wanted to captain the team from a young age.

While I didn't know it yet, they were quite angry when Mr. Bowman picked me for the team captain. There were only two sports in school, cricket and Australian Rules football, and both the team captains were considered very highly in school. They thought that one of them should have been appointed for the captaincy and I didn't have the right to that position.

The school was just a fifteen-minute walk away from my home down Waverly Road. I headed home at the end of the school day, quite happy and content with myself. But some of the boys had left early, run across the oval at the back of the school, and made their way through the back streets to cut me off on my way home. As I reached halfway to my house, I realized that boys from the school were standing on the footpath in front of me. There were three of them.

I started feeling a little bit nervous. I didn't know why the boys were standing on the footpath at a time like this, but the way that they were looking at me and waiting for me told me something was not right. They had taken their school bags off and were just standing there, waiting. I just kept my head down and kept walking towards home. I had to go past them to get home; there was no way around it. The closer I got to the three boys, the more nervous I became. I had known bullies in the past, and these guys looked like trouble.

As I walked past them, I said hello, but none of them responded.

The first boy, Michael, just approached me and said, "Who do you think you are?"

Scared and nervous, I said nothing.

The other boy, Craig, then stepped forward, looked me dead in the eyes and said, "You have no right being the cricket captain."

"I didn't pick the team captain. It was Mr. Bowman's decision," I replied.

The third boy didn't wait to say anything. He just swung his fist at me, and it connected with the side of my head, near the temple. I was stunned, not only from the blow but also by the suddenness of it all. I just stood there frozen and silent. Michael again stepped up to me and punched me right on the nose; it immediately started bleeding. The blood dripped down my nose and onto my shirt. Craig, not to be outdone, kicked me really hard in the shins.

I started to run. I just ran and ran, all the way down the street. Waverly Road was pretty busy; there were people driving past and residents in their front yards, but no one tried to intervene or said a word. They just watched as the boys chased me, yelling and swearing at me. I'm not a very fast runner, but I ran pretty fast that day. We lived on Waverly Road, and I managed to make it to my house without them catching me again. I burst through the front door and collapsed on the floor. Mum came rushing to pick me up and find out what was wrong.

"What happened to you?" she said as she wrapped her arms around me. "What's wrong?"

I couldn't speak to begin with. I just sat their crying while she held me. I wasn't sure I was ever going to stop sobbing. My nose hurt, my head hurt, and I never wanted to go to school ever again.

Mum got me up and took me into the kitchen to sit down at the table while she went and got the first aid kit from the laundry.

"You can tell me all about it in a minute," she said. "Let's get you all cleaned up first." She washed the blood off my face, made sure my nose had stopped bleeding, and then she sent me off to the bathroom to have a shower. She got me a fresh set of clothes, and once I was out of the shower and warm and dry, she sat me down on the couch in the lounge room.

"Tell me what happened," she said.

So, I told her the whole story. How I had been selected as the cricket captain, and how some of the team thought it should have been them, and they decided to get me and beat me up on the way home from school. As I described the walk home and how I felt seeing the three boys waiting for me on the road, I began to get upset again.

"I could tell this was going to be bad," I said to Mum. "I just knew as I walked towards them that they wanted to hurt me, but there was nowhere else for me to go. To get home, I had to go past them."

I told her the rest of the story, finishing with running home with the boys chasing me all the way. Mum gave me a hug, got the biscuits out for afternoon tea, and found me a book to read to try to rest. I was even allowed to eat in the lounge room, which never happened.

When Dad got home, I heard Mum telling him

what had happened. Dad then talked to me, and I filled in the details. Dad decided to write a letter to the school about it, reporting the three boys for assault. He gave the letter to me and told me to take it to school with me the next day and give it to Mrs. West.

The next morning, there was no hiding the bruises on my face and neck. I had a black eye and a lump on the right side of my head near the temple. Dad was pretty angry about how I had been treated, and this kind of encouraged me because I knew that he wasn't angry at me but *for* me. I knew my parents loved me, but having Dad angry at someone else because they had treated me badly made me feel loved and safe.

I took the letter to school and gave it to Mrs. West. She read the letter but said nothing at the time. During lunchtime, she asked me to stay back in the classroom after the other students had gone out to lunch and spoke with me. She told me that she had read the letter and seen the bruises on my face.

"This is unacceptable behaviour," she said, looking sorry that I was treated that way. "You can be assured that if the boys step out of line again, they will be unable to play on the cricket team for the rest of the year." While that sounded reasonable to me, I wanted to know what the consequences were for what they had already done. But none of the boys got any punishment that I knew about. I felt like the school was doing nothing at all to protect me.

In the next cricket game, Mr. Bowman, who knew

what had happened, made me the twelfth man for the team, even though I was the wicketkeeper and the team captain. This meant that I couldn't bat; I could only field, as the twelfth man was the substitute fielder. I fielded and thought I did an excellent job of it. Mr. Bowman had thought that by making me the twelfth man, he would take some of the heat out of the entire situation. But for me, it was the same as being punished. Not only did I have to take the beating, but I was also being punished for it too, demoted to twelfth man when I had done nothing wrong.

I had told my parents, and they had told the school, but still, I was the one being punished. I was the one missing out. I was still part of the team, but a minor one. Going from the team captain to the twelfth man was humiliating. They were showing me that even after being selected as the captain, I wasn't really part of the team.

So, I decided there and then to never complain about a bully ever again. There didn't seem to be much point to telling others about people's bad behaviour or bullying. I could speak up about it, about being attacked while going home, I could tell my parents and the school, but still, there wouldn't be any justice. I was the team captain still, and I wasn't the twelfth man in the other matches, but I never felt part of the team ever again. I never felt accepted in the team, or at school, for that matter.

I was all alone.

There was another boy in my class – his name was Jake. He had heard about what had happened to me, and he wasn't against me for taking the captaincy. Jake was the kind of kid who worked hard at school. He was big, tall, and fairly strong for his age. His father was a plasterer who worked in construction, and Jake used to help out whenever he could.

I tried to become friends with Jake. I felt like Jake might be someone who would be on my side and come to my aid when I was in trouble, like a protector. I still remembered Dad's advice for dealing with bullies was to pick the biggest one and make friends with them (although I still didn't know he'd also done the bully's homework). So, I picked Jake. In the class, all the boys were allowed to sit anywhere they wanted, but I always tried to sit next to Jake. I started to hang out with him at lunchtime and tried to make him a friend.

One day, the teacher surprised us with a maths test. Everyone got a sheet of paper, and they had to fill out the sheet with answers. The test comprised twenty questions. Over the next half hour, the class was busy trying to answer all the questions. When the time was up, Mrs. West told us to exchange papers with the person next to us. Mrs. West told us the correct answers, and everybody had to check their partner's papers and grade them. So, Jake got my test, and I got his.

As the teacher told the answers, I found out that I had done pretty well. I had got most of the answers right, and as I marked Jake's paper, I realized that he had got most of them wrong. In fact, out of all the twenty questions, Jake had only managed to get four right. When we had finished marking the papers, Mrs. West told us to raise our hands based on what marks the person whose paper they had checked had got. She started from the very top and told us to raise our hands if we had got twenty out of twenty.

No one raised their hands. After that came nineteen, again no one raised their hands. When the teacher came to eighteen, Jake put his hand up because I had got eighteen out of twenty. Still, no one else put their hands up. That meant that I had got the highest mark. Mrs. West kept going down the list. After she had gotten to six, she asked if anyone had gotten less than five marks.

Without even thinking about, it I raised my hand. No one else had put up their hands, and I was immediately sorry I had done that. The teacher asked me what the score was, and I told her that it was four. I was sitting right next to Jake, and he was pretty upset. The teacher asked Jake to stay behind after class and moved on. After class was over, everyone, including me, went for lunchtime while Jake stayed behind with the teacher. Around the middle of lunchtime, Jake came storming out of the classroom and made a beeline for me. He was very angry and looked like it.

"Why did you do it?" he asked furiously. "Why couldn't you keep your mouth shut? Why did you have to tell her anything? Look at what you've done. Now I have to stay after school and do extra homework, and it's all your fault."

I didn't know what to say. I wasn't really thinking. I just did what the teacher had told me to do, not knowing I was doing anything wrong. I certainly hadn't thought about the social implications of putting my hand up and telling the teacher what mark Jake got. Jake put the entire blame on me. He threatened to beat me up after school.

I had already been beaten up once by three boys, and Jake was bigger and stronger than everyone. This really frightened me. I knew that Jake was still angry and that he would probably beat me up the first chance he got. I had already learned that telling anyone would be a mistake. No one would listen, and then they would come up with a way to punish me instead.

For the rest of school that day, I had a sick, anxious feeling in the pit of my stomach. As school finished and the bell rang, I got up, packed my back, and headed out the classroom door to start walking home. Students from different year groups were hanging around in the courtyard chatting, and all the teachers had headed off to the staffroom, mingling and sharing stories about the day. The courtyard was unsupervised.

As headed towards the front gate to walk home, I felt a tap on my shoulder. I looked around, and it was Jake standing there.

"You're going to pay for what you did to me today."

And with that, Jake swung at me and punched me

on the nose. For the second time that year, it started bleeding, but this time it was different. This time, I knew that I was all alone and whatever was to be done, I would have to do it myself. So, I took a swing at Jake and punched him right in the stomach, which didn't have any effect at all. Jake just kept throwing punches at me from every side while I kept trying to defend myself and blocking the punches that were coming my way.

Just at that moment, I saw Mrs. West walk out of the classroom. She didn't come over our way, even though all the kids were gathered around us in a circle, watching and yelling. She just kept her head down and kept walking towards the staffroom. I couldn't believe it! How could she not see what was going on? I thought about running up to her and telling her everything. I was already bleeding, and I wanted this to end. I didn't think it wouldn't solve anything, but since I didn't have any more options at the time, I did it anyway.

I ran up to Mrs. West and got to her just before she went through the door into the staffroom. She broke up the fight and told Jake to go home. She told me that she would do something about it. And that was it. I didn't want to walk home, in case Jake was waiting for me around the corner, so I sat at school by myself for ages until I thought it was safe. Then I headed home.

This time, I didn't tell my parents; I sneaked in the front door, went into the bathroom, and cleaned up my nose as best I could. I put on my jumper so my parents wouldn't see anything and put my shirt under cold water. I soaked it just like Mum had shown me and kept doing it until there were no more bloodstains on it. To this day, I don't think my parents ever knew anything about the entire incident. The next morning, I got up and trudged off to school like it was any other day.

As the target of bullies, I felt powerless. It seemed to me that no one was prepared to hold the bully accountable for their actions; they just wanted to sweep things under the carpet and pretend it wasn't happening. Even when my parents made a fuss and did their best to stick up for me, nothing was done. So, it made sense to me that it would be better if I did the same thing. If no one was going to stop it from happening, then I had to learn how to live with it on my own.

7

Turbulent Chasm

I was in a sticky situation, and no matter how much I tried, it just kept getting worse. I was the captain of the cricket team, but that didn't mean anything. Twice I was beaten up because of something I did. The first time I told my story, it seemed like I was the one being punished. I told my parents, I told the teachers, and it didn't do me any good. The second time, I hid it from everyone.

This was one of the most difficult periods of my life. I didn't want to go to school, but I couldn't tell anyone about it. I was now always frightened about going to school. Jake beat me up, and I ran to the teacher and told her all about it. She promised me that she would do something about it. But again, as far as I could tell, nothing changed.

After that, I just stopped talking to my parents about anything happening at school. I stopped talking to the teachers about anything because every time I told someone that I was being bullied, things would just get worse. I was at a very low point in my life. I felt alone and ostracized and just kept to myself, even though I felt isolated. Every morning when I woke up for school, I had this horrible feeling in the pit of my stomach that I could not get rid of. I decided to be as quiet and as small as possible. I tried to stay out of everyone's way so no one would notice me.

The way I behaved, the way I acted in the class, everything just shifted. I tried my best to keep away from the bullies as much as I could. This became a bit more difficult when Mrs. West asked me to be the monitor for the school bell.

Jordanville South had a school bell that was rung at the beginning and end of each class, as well as at the start of recess and lunch, to let students and teachers know when a class had ended. Every few weeks, a different student from the sixth grade would be given the responsibility of ringing the bell. They would keep their eyes on the clock on the classroom wall, and when it was time, they would leave the class a little bit early and press the button to ring the bell.

Halfway through the school year, I was given this privilege. Mrs. West didn't give this privilege to just anyone, so it was considered very cool to have this important responsibility. It also meant you got to leave early at the end of every single lesson to ring the bell.

When I was given this task, I was very diligent

with it; I kept my eyes on the clock because I didn't want to make any mistakes. I would make sure that the bell rang exactly on time. I knew that if I rang the bell at the wrong time, I'd lose out and no longer be able to leave class early to ring it. Usually, a student would get this job for a couple of weeks, and then Mrs. West would nominate someone else for it.

There weren't enough weeks for every student in the sixth grade to have a go. Only the kids who were well behaved in the class would get this job as a reward. Unfortunately, when I was given this responsibility, it meant that another student in my class missed out. There were some kids in the class who felt like it was another one of those privileges that should be reserved for students who had been in the school much longer than me.

I did this task for a few days without any incident. By the time Friday came, at the end of recess, three boys from the class decided that they would stop me from ringing the bell.

These boys stood in front of the school office where I had to ring the bell, and they waited for me. I went up to the office a couple of minutes before recess ended, as usual, and I saw the boys just standing there. I sensed that something was wrong, so as I walked up to the door, I tried to avoid eye contact and pretend they weren't there.

They took me by the shoulders and pushed me back, holding me hard so I wouldn't get away. I tried my

best to get away from them and go do what I was supposed to do. It was my responsibility, and I took it very
seriously. They not only kept pushing me back but also
abused me with their words. *You don't deserve this. You
have gone on long enough. This will stop,* and more.

I tried to push my way through them, and they
pushed me to the ground, flat on my back. At this time,
a teacher walked past the office. He immediately saw
what was going on and told the boys to leave me alone
and go back to their classes. I went in and rang the bell,
and the teacher walked away. Once again, the bullies did
not get what they deserved. There was no punishment
at all for them. They were just told off, and things went
on the way they were going. There was no detention
or picking up rubbish in the playground during lunch.
I had a hard time understanding why there were never
any consequences for my bullies. I think it was just part
of the culture of the school, and the teachers either
didn't know it was going on or didn't know how to stop
it in such a difficult school and just turned a blind eye to
it.

As the year went on, it got cold and wet. Winter was upon us, and in Melbourne, that meant lots of
clouds and cold winds. About halfway through second
term, it seemed like we'd had a few weeks of this in
a row. It was Monday, and we were looking at another
week just like the last one.

I arrived at school and went into class. Each
morning, we had a spelling test of the memory words
we had been given the day before, but I wasn't inter-

ested. Our classroom wasn't heated, so the wet and cold atmosphere made it one of those dreary days that seem like they will never end. By the end of second period, most of the students had already stopped listening to Mrs. West; we were just waiting for the lunch period. Finally, the bell went off, and the whole class rushed out the door. It was cold, and the wind made me shiver as I made my way out of the classroom and headed towards the canteen for lunch.

Buying lunch was a rare privilege in those days. Mum usually packed me a frozen Vegemite-and-cheese sandwich that would be made a few weeks in advance. She'd give it to me every day straight out of the freezer, and it would thaw in my lunchbox every morning. But today was one of those special days when Mum had run out of sandwiches and had a few spare coins so I could buy lunch at school.

The canteen was on the other side of the school from our grade six classroom, so the lucky ones among us started to head towards the canteen. It was also where cola-flavoured Sunny Boys and all the lollies that we could afford to buy awaited us. As I took my usual shortcut to the canteen, right between the admin building and the library, I felt two hands grab me from behind. They pinned my arms behind my back and held on tight while someone roped something around my neck.

I kicked my left leg backward and tried to free my arms, but their hold wouldn't loosen up. A sinking feeling of panic swirled in my stomach, swimming through my veins, muscles, and right up my throat, where the wire was being tightened dangerously. The utter panic and fear made me freeze up and locked my body in place. I could hear their loud, taunting laughter in my ears as I began to thrash my arms back and forth in a fight to save myself. I tried to elbow the kid behind me. I then grabbed and pulled on the wire, and it loosened enough to give me some breathing space.

Then I kicked my legs behind me and hit one of the boys where it hurts, right in the nuts. The boy collapsed on the ground in pain, and I took that chance to pull the wire away from my neck. I threw the wire down and ran out from between the buildings, heading for the canteen, breathing hard and doing my best to not look as panicked as I really felt.

Even though I was extremely frightened, I tried to remain calm and pretend like it was just another day. I was sure I looked like I had been in a fight and had a clear mark around my neck, and I was very upset and agitated. I pushed all those feelings down. I tried my best not to cry and not to show any external emotions. I knew that nobody was going to help me and that I was completely on my own. The best way that I knew to deal with it was to pretend it never happened.

Gradually, I slowed down; my running turned into a walk. I arrived at the canteen and bought some Ovalteenies. I also got a drink and found a quiet spot. I sat down there, trying to calm my nerves. I still don't know how I could appear calm after such a horrific incident, but I managed somehow. I could not show anything on the outside. Nobody would help me, and nobody was ever going to be by my side. I knew that I had to do everything alone.

The next day, I got up, and I had a feeling of fear in the pit of my stomach. I woke up covered in sweat from a bad dream. The last thing I wanted to do was go to school. I tried to fool Mum into thinking I was sick so I could stay home. But Mum was a nurse before she had us kids and was hard to fool.

So, I got up slowly, I got dressed slowly, and I ate breakfast slowly. I walked to school slowly, anything I could do to make myself late, so I had as little time as possible at that terrible place. But each step to get ready kept on coming; it was inevitable. There was no avoiding school that day, no matter how hard I tried.

The next day began the same way, and the next and the next and the next. That horrible feeling when I woke up, followed by doing everything I could to avoid having to go to school. I would argue with my parents, pretend to be sick, pick fights with Matt, complain about anything and everything. I would have done anything I could to stay home. The closer it got to the time I had to leave to walk to school, I would feel panicked, hot, and sweaty, no matter how cold it was outside.

When I eventually got to school, I did my best to bury all those feelings as deep inside as I could and just get through it. I never wanted anyone to know how I was feeling, especially no one at school. I felt so incredibly alone, it was like I was living in a bubble. I was inside my own little world, and within it I was completely by myself. The world went on outside my bubble, but the bubble wasn't there to protect me. Instead, it was the place everyone else had put me in, as if I wasn't good enough to be a part of the real world, I was only good enough to live inside my bubble separated from everyone else.

Some days I felt like I was outside of my own body, floating up above myself and just watching what was going on below me like some kind of movie. I could see myself sitting in class and answering a question when I was asked, but it was like it wasn't really me. It was someone else down there being me. I was just an observer, watching from a safe distance.

To keep myself safe, I started asking the teachers if I could go to the library during lunchtime, just like I did at my last school. I knew that it was one of the safest places in the school. The boys were all playing sports outside, and nobody was interested in going to the library during lunchtime. It was a good space for me, protected and safe.

I didn't know it then, but I have learnt that my reaction to these experiences were not unusual for a survivor of physical and psychological abuse. Withdrawing from others, going to safe places, keeping quiet while a part of groups, and trying not to draw attention to myself were all symptoms of what happened to me at Jordanville South. By the end of that year, I was timid, scared, and my heart had been broken.

8

Doors Opening, Doors Closing

Finally, graduation day at Jordanville South arrived. We had a graduation lunch with all of the school's teachers, we said our farewells, and off we went. I was leaving this awful year behind and heading off to high school, and I was looking forward to it very much. Nothing could be worse than the past year at Jordanville South Primary. After everything that had happened, a new school was exactly what I needed. I hoped that this change would help me find a place for myself, make some new friends, experience different opportunities, and meet new teachers. I was a little bit hopeful and a little bit anxious – optimistic because I wanted it to work, nervous because I was afraid it wouldn't.

In the beginning, high school went pretty well. I made three new friends, Andrew, Mark, and Paul. Andrew played tennis, and he was also featured on TV as an up-and-coming star. Mark was pretty smart and was keen on going to a selective high school in a couple of years. We all used to sit together in class, work together, and spend our time chatting and talking. We became pretty good mates. Paul was a little bit different from the rest. He was a bit of a loner, but he was also a bit of a prankster. He loved playing practical jokes on others. One time, he brought fart gas to school and let it go in the hallway. All the teachers and students were around, and it was pretty hilarious the way everyone was gagging from the smell and struggling to get away from it.

I had a lot of fun with Paul; in fact, I had a lot of fun with all the guys. We became fast friends, and I started to enjoy high school. I started listening to music. I really loved bands like INXS, Kids in the Kitchen, and U2. The more I listened, the more I talked about it with my friends. My grades got better too. In the first few terms, I started getting As again, except for French. I wasn't a huge fan of French. And I was not too fond of geography either. The teacher was very strict, and I wasn't a fan. So, I didn't work hard enough on these two subjects. Apart from these, I was excelling at all the other subjects. Life was good.

In the first term, I was selected to be a part of the school cricket team as the wicketkeeper. We won every game we played against the other schools in our district and won the final. We had a very good team. We made the regional competition semi-final, but we lost that game fairly convincingly. But I loved it. I had never been part of a winning team in any sport before.

After the cricket season finished, Andrew had his birthday, and he invited the whole team. It was on a Saturday at his house; it started in the afternoon and went till dinnertime. I was really looking forward to it. Andrew had a swimming pool at his house, so we all brought our bathers and were keen for a swim. Paul didn't play sports and wasn't really friends with Andrew and Mark, so he wasn't invited.

I arrived a bit late to the party, and it was already going well. I jumped in the pool for a swim, and Andrew's dad cooked lunch on the BBQ while we dive bombed each other, took spectacular catches with a tennis ball while jumping in the pool, and basically enjoyed ourselves.

When the cooking on the BBQ was done, we hopped out of the pool and began to eat. There were twelve of us at the party, guys and girls sitting around chatting. Erica, one of the girls in the group, told us that Paul had asked her out on a date, and she was making fun of him for it, explaining how awkward he was and how she wasn't interested in him at all. Mark and Andrew soon joined the conversation and started criticizing Paul and picking on him. They laughed at him for his antics. They were talking about him like he was an idiot. They made fun of his hair, his looks, and the way he conducted himself. I tried to keep out of it, but Paul was my friend, and the more they talked, the angrier I got. And finally, I was uncomfortable enough and angry enough to speak up.

"That's enough!" I said, much louder than I intended to. "Paul is a good guy. Making fun of people behind their back is not on." I got up and walked away from the group to calm down. I felt a bit embarrassed that I had reacted that way and anxious about what was going to happen next. However, it all seemed to blow over. Everyone finished eating and then headed home as our parents picked us up at the end of the party.

On Monday I headed off to school. I had basically forgotten about what had happened at the party and was on my way to class when I overheard Mark and Andrew talking in the corridor just around the corner from me.

"What was going on with Josiah at your party?" asked Mark.

"I don't know," said Andrew. "I think Josiah was overreacting. We didn't mean any harm."

I walked around the corner carrying my books under my left arm. As I walked past them, Andrew reached out and flipped my books out from under my arm so they went crashing down onto the floor. My pens and notes went everywhere all over the floor. Mark and Andrew headed off to class thinking this was a great laugh, and I was left to pick everything up on my own.

One of the hardest parts of being bullied in the past is it doesn't take much to bring those feelings up again. Even though Mark and Andrew weren't really trying to bully me, they thought it was a great joke and a bit of payback for what I had said at the party. In that moment, all I could feel was the humiliation of having to get down on the floor and pick up everything, while other students around me hurried off to class.

As I was picking up those papers, the feelings I used to have about school came flooding back. The awful fear from the pit of my stomach returned, and when I had picked everything up and arrived in class, instead of sitting at a desk with Mark like I normally would have, I went and sat at the back at a desk on my own.

So, from that day onwards, I started hanging out mostly with Paul. We sat next to each other in level-one mathematics class. We would compete and try to answer the questions faster and finish the work before each other. We both enjoyed hanging out together, but we were cut off from the rest of the group. At least I wasn't alone this time.

The more I hung out with Paul, the more I learned about him. He wasn't just a practical joker at school; he was also involved with activities outside of school that most parents would disapprove of. One of the things that he liked to do was shoplifting. Like me, he had grown up in a low-income family. They never had a lot of stuff. He was living with his mother, and his father was not around.

Paul had saved up enough cash to buy a Commodore 64 home computer. In those days, it was around $460, and that was a considerable sum for a thirteen-year-old boy to collect. But he managed to do it. He brought it home and set it up in his bedroom. I used to go to his house, and we would play games all day long. It had a tape drive, not a floppy drive, and the games would take ten minutes to load. Our favourite game was called Galaga. Another one was called F1 American Strike Eagle. You flew an American warplane and shot down other enemy aircraft. We played those games for hours on end.

Paul and I would go out together to different stores and find games that we liked. We would take those games and bring them home; we called it the five-fingered discount. One time, we went to Myers, and we wanted to buy a game called Mortal Kombat. We walked into the store, and Paul was the one tasked with picking up the game and putting it in my pocket. I kept a lookout for security cameras and store managers and assistants. We were successful and took the game home.

I knew that these were not good things to do and that my parents would never want me to do this. I clearly remembered back in Loxton when I was caught shoplifting with Barry. But I had no other way of bonding with Paul, and I had no friends otherwise, so I joined in. I had learned a long time ago that if I wanted to be friends with people, I needed to become like them. It's not a good way to live and make decisions in the long term, but at the time, that's how things felt to me.

Around that time, I got a job at the local news-agent delivering newspapers. I delivered newspapers door to door, in the early morning. I reached the newsagent at five o'clock in the morning, picked up my load of papers, and delivered them to different streets. After I finished, I rode back to the shop to give my report. I did this six days a week, two hours each morning, earning a sum of $17.50 from the newsagent every week. It was cash in hand, and for me, it was a considerable amount. I was very proud of my job. I got to work in a real-life environment, and I had my own money to spend and buy things that I wanted.

One of the things that I wanted was a pair of baggy jeans. They had come out in the '80s, were quite loose, and had big pockets on the sides and button pockets at the shins. They gathered at the ankles. I thought they were the coolest things I had ever seen, and I wanted a pair. So, I saved up my money from my job and bought myself a pair. I wasn't allowed to wear them to school as we had a uniform, but I wore them everywhere else. I wore them as much as possible.

But I wasn't satisfied with earning money and saving up for the things I wanted. In fact, after a while, I began stealing what I wanted on my own. I had started stealing with Paul because it made me feel accepted, but I got used to having more of the things other kids did, and it became a habit. The more I did it, the less I worried about getting caught or if it was wrong or not. My conscience went quiet.

My love of computers led me to steal books about them from the local library. The library would only let you borrow a book for fourteen days. That made no sense to me, as some of these books had hundreds of programs, written in the BASIC computer code, that I could use to program the school computer. Fourteen days was never going to be enough time to go program them all. I would bring them home and then sneak them into school so I could use the books to write programs for the Commodore 64.

I began steal from the news agency where I worked as well. I was a big fan of Phantom comics and began to steal them from work, as well as Tic-Tacs one of my favourite sweets. One morning I put a whole package of them in my newspaper bag and sneaked them out the front door of the newsagent right under my boss Andy's nose! There were forty boxes of Tic-Tacs wrapped up in one big package. Talk about a sugar high!

One day, my mother found the books that I had stolen from the library. I told ger that I had taken them from the library and "forgot" to borrow them properly, but Mum was too smart for that and made me take the books back to the library and confess to taking them, which was very embarrassing for me. I told Mum that Paul and I had done it together (I was always pretty honest once I was caught) so she called Paul's mother and told her what Paul and I had done.

The next day, when I got to school, Paul wouldn't talk to me. He told me that we were no longer friends. He was tremendously angry that I had brought him into it. For a couple of weeks, we stayed this way. We didn't talk, and when I tried to explain it to him, he didn't want to listen. Finally, he did listen and respond, but instead of admitting that we were doing something wrong, he started telling me I was a fool to keep the books in the open where anybody could find them.

Paul told me that I had to be careful and that I should have done better. We had barely gotten over the fight when my father discovered the Phantom comic books under my bed. I had ripped the covers off them and folded quite a few of the pages them to make them look older than they were in a vain attempt to convince my parents they weren't new and a friend had loaned them to me.

But my father worked it out, and once again I found myself confessing. My father marched me down to the newsagent to tell my boss what I had done. The feeling I had walking to see Andy was pretty horrid. It was a twenty-five-minute walk, and the whole way, I just begged my dad to do all the talking for me, but he told me I would have to do the talking myself, as it was my responsibility.

My stomach was turning upside down as we walked. I felt like throwing up and just wanted to turn around and run in the opposite direction as fast as I could. But instead, I just kept plodding along next to Dad, doing my best to pretend on the outside I was per-fectly fine.

We arrived at the news agency, opened the door, and walked in carrying the pile of Phantom comics. Andy, who was about my dad's age, looked down at me and said, "Well, what have we here? That's a big pile of comics. Where did they come from?"

I stayed silent and just stood there till my dad tapped me on the shoulder, indicating that I needed to speak.

"Ahhhhh, ummmm, well they come from here," I said.

"Do they?" said Andy. "I don't remember selling you any comic books. How did you get them?"

I was desperate not say I had stolen them, so I said, "Well, I took them but forgot to pay for them."

"He stole them," my father added.

At this point, I wanted to fade into the floor and disappear. Andy was such a good and kind boss who was always friendly and concerned about his paperboys.

"Well, how about we just put them back on the shelf and forget all about it," said Andy. "I am sure you have learnt your lesson, haven't you, Josiah?"

"That won't work," I stammered. "They have been damaged."

Andy took the pile of comics from me and looked them over.

"You're right," he said. "I can't sell these." He thought about it for a moment, and then he said, "I think you have learned your lesson, and I am not going to fire you, but I need you to repay the cost of the comics, and I think I should keep them rather than give them back to you."

"Okay," I managed to reply.

Andy put the comics behind the counter, said thanks to my dad for bringing me down there, and told me he would see me tomorrow. Andy decided to take the money I owed him out of my wages each week until I had paid it back.

I thought that I would get fired, and I heaved a sigh of relief when that didn't happen. I found out years later that my father was hoping that I *would* get fired, to teach me a lesson. But I had to keep working and pay for the comics from my weekly wages. I had stolen thirty-four comics from him, and they were around two dollars each. It took me over a month to pay it off.

I decided there and then that I would never steal anything again! I don't know why Andy was so kind to me, but he cured me of stealing through that kindness.

9

Shift Happens

At the end of 1986, our time in Melbourne was over, and my family relocated to Canberra. My father had been appointed the pastor of a church in North Canberra, and we all moved up to the nation's capital city.

Canberra in 1987 was a growing city that had more than doubled in size over the previous twenty years to just over 250,000 people. In Australia, that's a large rural city, but much smaller than Melbourne and way more relaxed. People in Canberra loved Rugby League, Australian Rules Football, cricket, and basketball. And even though I had no idea what Rugby League was, it felt much more like home than Melbourne ever had.

My parents decided to enrol Matt and me in different schools, so I found myself starting year nine at Canberra High. I had no idea what the school was like, if I would be able to make friends, or if I would be bullied again. But the one thing I did know is that I would never steal again.

I wasn't going to try to fit into the crowd anymore. I had a new start, and I wanted to make different choices about what I was going to do with my life and my behaviour. So, the move to Canberra was a good thing for me, as it gave me the chance to transition. I could leave all my troubles behind in Melbourne and make a fresh start.

The church Dad was working at provided us with a house to live in, and on the first Sunday after we moved, we headed off to meet this new bunch of people our family was becoming a part of. While our family had always gone to church, it hadn't had much meaning for me over the previous few years. I knew all the right answers I was supposed to give at church, but I wasn't sure what I really thought about God. For a start, God hadn't prevented me from being bullied, and that hardly seemed fair. In fact, sometimes it seemed that going to church was one of the things that made me an easy target. It wasn't exactly a cool thing to do.

That first Sunday was interesting. Not so much the church bit, but there was a couple of girls my age who I decided I would like to get to know. After the service was finished, my dad had brought a few boxes of books in our van to bring into his office. I happily volunteered to get them out of the car, I figured carrying boxes of books would impress these girls somehow. But they took no notice, proving once again I still had no idea what I was doing.

The church had a youth group that met on Friday nights, and as the pastor's kid, it was expected I would go along, but I was actually looking forward to it. There were plenty of people my age, and it looked like fun – what they called a reverse progressive dinner.

A progressive dinner meant going to a different person's house for each part of a meal. One house for the entrée, one for the main course, and a different house again for dessert. A reverse progressive dinner was done in reverse. You started with dessert and finished with the entrée, oh, and you had to wear all your clothes backwards.

So, we all met at the church and then walked to the first person's house for dessert, which sounded like a great plan to me. Fancy getting to eat dessert first! When we arrived at the house and opened the door, I met Mrs. Middleweek for the first time, and I was astonished.

The other kids in the group had told me we were going to one of the youth leaders' houses, but here stood Mrs. Middleweek, and she had to be at least sixty! How could she possibly be one of the youth leaders? In my limited experience, youth leaders in churches were often just a few years older than the kids they led. I was expecting someone close to my age, but Mrs. Middleweek was almost twice my dad's age.

I managed to keep a reasonably straight face and not overreact, and we all walked into Mrs. Middleweek's house in our terribly uncomfortable clothes, which were, of course, all on backwards. Dessert was outstanding, my favourite, lemon meringue pie! Mrs. Middleweek just became my favourite youth leader of all time. Everyone knows the way to a young boy's heart is through his stomach!

As the dinner progressed, I got to know Mrs. Middleweek, and she was actually pretty cool. Our group walked from one house to the next for the main course and then the entrée, and Mrs. Middleweek was pretty fit and kept up with us no problem. She was a good talker and seemed interested in me and my experiences.

As the weeks passed, each Friday I looked forward to youth group, not only because I was getting to know some of the other people who went, but because Mrs. Middleweek always seemed keen to listen to what I had to say. I really liked it, and it encouraged me a lot.

I found Mrs. Middleweek to be quite different from any of the other older people I had met. My own grandparents were pretty distant. My grandfather on my dad's side had died when I was only thirteen, and my grandfather on my mum's side had died years before I was born. My grandma on Mum's side I had only met a couple of times. And my grandma on my mum's side didn't seem to understand me or Matt very well. They were also all in South Australia, which is a long way from Canberra.

Mrs. Middleweek knew how to make a young person feel important. When she was listening, you knew that her entire focus was on you. She gave you her complete attention. She also let me know that she understood what I was saying. She was one of those people who knew how to help you feel safe, that you could trust her with your thoughts and fears.

One of the best things about her was that our swearing, bad jokes, and funny stories didn't upset her. She took it as calmly as ever. She knew exactly how to earn my trust. When I talked to her, she never once said anything or did anything that indicated she found what I said to be unimportant. I gradually started opening up to her, telling her about my time in Melbourne and the treatment I received at school. I even told her the truth about my shoplifting, stealing computer games and comics!

Mrs. Middleweek never once made me feel bad for doing the wrong thing. She wasn't judgey. She seemed happy to listen, and for me, she was a breath of fresh air. She had quite an impact on me. I felt like I had value, that I was being accepted for who I was. I didn't have to pretend to be someone I was not.

Despite this acceptance, I was still very uncertain about making friends with people my own age. Trusting one person is very different to making friends. At school I was still a bit of a loner, I had decided that keeping to myself was the best way to avoid encountering another bully. At the church's youth group, it seemed safer. But I was still very cautious. I didn't want to end up being bullied again, and I didn't know who to trust.

After a few months of attending youth group and getting to know people a bit, I had an idea. It seemed to me that there were some key things that popular kids all had in common. They tended to dress well, they had a sense of humour, and a big personality that people found interesting and wanted to be around. I decided that the best way to make friends would be to copy the most popular guy in the group.

We had about forty teenagers of high school age who came regularly. There were a few guys and girls who were well known in the youth group, but there was one who stood out amongst all the others. His name was Jonathan.

Jonathan was always the centre of attention. He was funny, told great stories, and people gravitated towards him. If Jonathan was interested in doing something, others were keen to join in.

So, I began to copy Jonathan's behaviour, to teach myself how to be liked. For example, when Jonathan laughed at someone else's jokes, he had a unique laugh. It was kind of high-pitched for a bloke, and sometimes people would laugh at the way Jonathan laughed, rather than just reacting to the story he had told. So, I began to copy Jonathan's laugh. It sounded a bit different, but the principle was the same. Your laugh had to grab the attention of the people listening to your story, with your own laugh at the end because it seemed to make others laugh too.

I started to try to tell funny stories of my own,

often making them up from scratch and basing them on the story Jonathan had just told. This would often happen after church when we were chatting as a group. I remember one story in particular.

Jonathan had been camping the week before with Boys Brigade, a Christian youth movement that had been so successful in the nineteenth century that it had led to the foundation of Scouts in England a decade or so after Boys Brigade began.

As part of the camp, they had to bring their own food and cook it on an open fire. Jonathan had taken with him a few cans of baked beans, which could be heated up by setting them on the hot plate over the campfire before opening them up and eating them straight from the can with a spoon.

On the last day of camp, he had one can left. So, Jonathan decided to put this can of baked beans on the hot plate and leave it there to see what would happen when the can overheated. He got up early in the morning before anyone else was awake, stoked up the fire, put the can of baked beans on the hot plate, hid behind a nearby tree, and waited.

As a group, we were all focused on Jonathan as he told this story; he had our full attention.

"I waited behind the tree for what seemed like ages," he whispered, and we all leaned in to hear what he was going to say. "I got to the point of thinking nothing was going to happen, when there was this massive bang!" he said as he clapped his hands together. "I looked out from behind the tree, and the can was gone! The other campers and leaders had all come rushing out of their tents at the massive noise. They were all looking around with no idea what had happened. It was hilarious," he said, laughing so hard that we all felt compelled to join in. And it was a funny moment to imagine.

So, I jumped in with my own story. I made it different enough. In my story, it was a can of spaghetti rather than baked beans, and I was on an Explorers Camp in the Grampians. It was a gas BBQ rather than an open fire, and it was at night instead of in the morning. In my story, the can exploded and sent spaghetti all over the campsite, covering the tents, people's chairs, and their shoes outside their tents. The spaghetti went everywhere.

Of course, my story was completely made up, but I told it as if it was true, and everyone laughed along with me, just as they had with Jonathan. Even though I wasn't really being myself, I was just trying to be like the most popular person in the group, it felt good to get a positive response like that. I didn't care the story wasn't true; they were never going to find that out, and I was learning how to build social connections with others, which is what I was trying to achieve.

This method of mine began to work. I started to feel more important in the group. Others began to listen to my stories. I even told ones that were actually true, and I was starting to feel safer and trust this group of people more.

It was a process of trial and error, though. On our church camp that year, I was talking with one of the girls in our group, and I made a joke that really offended her because it was at her expense. I don't really want to repeat the joke here because it wasn't nice. That horrid feeling in the pit of my stomach, which I'd learned was called anxiety, came flooding back. I felt like a grade-six kid being bullied all over again, except it was me who was being horrible to someone else. Which somehow made it much worse, because even though I had apologised to her, I had caused someone else the kind of pain I used to feel every single day.

Despite a few more setbacks, I was slowly learning some social skills. Jonathan and I became good friends over time. After church, myself and others from our youth group would often head over to Jonathan's house for fish and chips, and I learned how to make an awesome chip sandwich, (bread, tomato sauce, a lot of chips, and a couple of slices of cheese – it was a beautiful thing).

About this time, the guys in our youth group put together a basketball team. It was called the CCs. We used to play every week in the ACT basketball competition. It really became something that I enjoyed, not because I was a great basketball player, I was average, but because as a team competing together, we accepted each other and worked together to achieve something greater than we could ever achieve on our own. So, I started playing more and more.

The thing that really gave me an advantage over other players was my height. I played as the centre, and soon I became a decent defender. I never scored a lot of points; in many games I didn't score any points at all, but I was really good at stopping our opposition from scoring and quickly became quite successful. The more I played, the better I became, and the better I became, the more I started to relax and enjoy it. I gained a bit more confidence, and it all helped. I had found something that other people recognized me as being good at.

Was I the greatest basketball player in the world? By no means. I knew that I would never play professional basketball or anything like that. But I was good enough to contribute to the team, help them stop the opposition from scoring, and win games.

One of the things that our youth group did regularly was go on camps. There were three big camps we attended, Easter Camp, State Youth Games, and Blackstump. Usually about thirty to fifty young people from church would travel together to these camps. We had a great time making friends with people from other churches all around the ACT and NSW.

State Youth Games was held during the queen's birthday long weekend in Wollongong, NSW. Around a thousand young people from all over NSW and the ACT would gather for the weekend and compete against each other in a range of sports. We played basketball, soccer, athletics, touch football, tennis, table tennis, and many more.

I loved State Youth Games. There were aspects of it that made me nervous. I was away from home and meeting a lot of new people, and I had to reply on others for transport, so there were a lot of things I wasn't in control of. The fun of the weekend seemed to outweigh any nerves I felt.

There was also something different about this competition. When playing competitively against each other, there was no trash talk, no gloating when a team won, and if someone got injured, everyone jumped in to help, even the opposition players. Everyone wanted to participate and win, but each of the teams and individual players were good sports about it. In school sports or other competitions I had played in, winning and losing determined how much fun it was. At State Youth Games, it was fun, even when we were losing!

I took part in a table tennis competition, and I did pretty well in it. I played basketball with my team, and we won a few games to reach the finals. I tried to take part in as many sports as I could over the weekend. I played a couple of games of touch football, and when playing soccer, we made the grand final.

For the first time in my life, I felt like I had found a group of people who accepted me. The problem was I knew deep down that I had acted out a role, copying the most popular guy in our youth group. So even though I felt accepted, I knew deep down that no one really knew the real me. My inner fear still remained that if this new group knew the real me, instead of the person I pretended to be, I would be rejected all over again. So, while I started to find a bit of self-confidence, it was fragile and based on trying to fake it till I made it. And then I met Sonya.

Sonya loved playing basketball and netball. One afternoon after church, Sonya invited me to join her mixed netball team, with guys and girls playing on the same team. I had always thought netball was a bit of a girl's game, but Sonya was pretty convincing, so I decided to join the team.

The first game I played, I had no idea about the rules of the game. I was used to playing basketball, which is quite different from netball. For example, in basketball, the players can run wherever they want to on the court, and there are no set positions that players are assigned as part of the rules of the game. In netball, players can only go on the parts of the court their position allows them to.

I was pretty tall, so in that first game, I was given the position of goalkeeper. The goalkeeper must stay in the defensive third of the court and defend against the opposition's goal shooter. I quickly learned I was no good at this role. I didn't know where I was supposed to stand, how to defend well, and the opposition team kept scoring and scoring while I tried desperately to figure out what I was supposed to be doing.

The next week, I tried playing goalkeeper again but was failing miserably. So, at halftime, the coach moved me to the opposite end of the court to play goal shooter. Here was a role I knew how to play. I didn't have to worry about the rules covering defenders; basically, all I had to do was catch the ball that was passed to me and shoot it through the hoop.

I discovered that in netball, just like in basketball, my size gave me a lot of advantages on the court. I was taller than most of the defensive players, which meant I could receive a pass very close to the hoop, and it made the task of shooting goals much easier. As a team, from that game onwards, we played through the rest of the season undefeated. I had never expected to win a trophy playing netball (or any sport, really), but it looked good on the bookcase I had at home in my room regardless.

Sonya was a really good friend to me and very accepting. She always made me feel welcome, made me feel part of the team. She would pick me up, as she was a licensed driver, and I didn't drive. She picked me up from home, and we would just drive around and chat and hang out. We played netball and headed back home again.

At school, I still struggled to find my place. I wasn't being bullied the way I had been in Melbourne, but I still found it an uncomfortable place to be because of my own irrational thoughts that came from those past experiences. When I experienced a situation that brought back feelings of anxiety or worry, I would make adjustments to avoid the chance of feeling that anxiety again.

One big adjustment I had to make was to how I

travelled home from school each day. For the first half of the year, when I caught the bus home from school, I had to catch two busses, one from school to the bus interchange and then one from the bus interchange home. The bus from the school to the bus interchange was only for students, and it was always packed full. I would sit near the front, where I usually sat, and when a group of students laughed at the back of the bus, I would worry that it was me they were making fun of. Not very rational thinking, but after what I had experienced in my previous schools, it was an understandable fear.

To avoid feeling like this, I gave up catching the school bus and I decided to walk from the school to the interchange. I had to walk pretty fast to make sure I still caught my bus home to my house, but it meant I didn't have to sit on the bus and worry about whether the other students on the bus were laughing at me. I also got to spend the thirty cents I saved each day on the bus trip at the canteen at school!

10

Just Like Paradise

A year passed by after moving to Canberra, and I was now in year ten. One of my dreams at the time was to put together a band. I had been asked to sing in church a few times, and that was okay, but one of my dreams was to sing in a band Van Halen style. I had always been interested in music and had piano lessons for a while in Loxton, but it was singing that I was good at. At my previous schools, I was never confident enough to sing in front of people or try to put a group together, but with the confidence I had gained in church, I was more willing to have a go and take a risk, especially if it meant more people might think positively about me.

So, when it came time to choose our electives for the year, I picked music. There I met another great teacher by the name of Mrs. Powell. She too was a friendly and encouraging teacher, and I learned a lot from her. She kind of reminded me of Mrs. McGinn, my teacher in grade five. I had never forgotten her and probably never will. She was the first great teacher I ever had. Mrs. Powell was just like that too. She was kind and friendly and was always around for us. She encouraged me to try new things.

In music class, I made a new friend named Dave, who played the keyboard. He and I got on pretty well. We would play music together and discuss bands; he was a huge Pseudo Echo fan. The school year was broken up into three terms, and at the end of each term, the music class would give a performance in the school hall. It was a pretty big event. The parents of the students would be there, the principal and the teachers would be there, as well as other students and their brothers and sisters. During the term, our class would prepare individual and group performances and perform them in front of a crowd of about 350 people.

Dave was keen to join and play keys; we spoke to Steve, who played guitar, and he was keen too. Sheryn played drums, and we also had Michael on bass. Dave was such a great keyboard player, he didn't read music. If he had heard the song, he could work out how to play it. At the end of first term, we performed two songs by U2, and they went pretty well. At the end of second term, we picked a couple of songs, one by INXS and one by Bon Jovi. But the concert at the end of third term was the big one. It was usually attended by over five hundred people and was a big focus for the whole school. As school finished at the end of year ten and then students went to college, the end-of-year music performance by the year-ten class was the event that finished both the year and our time at the school. Everyone turned up for it.

Our band was playing two songs, "Just Like Paradise" by David Lee Roth and "Jump" by Van Halen. All through the term, we worked hard learning the songs, working out our arrangements and making sure it was going to be a really tight performance. I had more work than most, as I was performing with the band, and then I had my own solo performance as well later in the event.

The day finally arrived. The hall was packed solid full of teachers, students, and their families, The stage was set up, the sound system ready to go. The concert started, and everything was going great. Students were coming on stage to perform what they had prepared, and the audience was loving it. Soon it would be our turn to perform. We picked up our instruments and waited behind the curtain as the student before us (who was singing "You're the Voice" by John Farnham) finished singing and the curtains closed.

We walked out onto the stage, plugged in our instruments, and I picked up the microphone, ready to begin our first song, "Just Like Paradise." I nodded to Mrs. Powell that we were ready, and she pushed the button to open the curtain. The lights were dazzling, and the spotlight was on me. Sheryn, our drummer, counted us in, and Steve, Dave, and Michael began to play the intro.

It was a disaster. Steve's guitar sounded horrible. It was terribly out of tune and completely put me off as I was about to sing the first line of the song. I started to sing the first verse, but it was almost impossible to sing in the right key because Steve's guitar was ridiculously out of tune.

Mrs. Powell left her seat in the front row and walked up to the stage and told us to stop playing. She knew that something had gone wrong, and that we just couldn't go on playing with the guitar sounding that bad. Steve hurriedly tried to tune his guitar and start playing again, but the break in music caused a whole new problem. The audience were starting to create a ruckus. The students and other teenagers in the audience were shouting and yelling and making fun of us while Steve tried to fix his guitar and the rest of us waited. They were picking on us and making fun of our band.

As the yelling and shouting became louder, it pushed Steve to his limits, and he was incredibly frustrated. He got upset with the crowd and yelled into the microphone for them to shut up. Up till that point, it was still manageable, but then it began to get out of hand. Steve, in a moment of frustration and anger, got the bright idea to give the audience the bird.

That's when the principal stepped in. He was sitting in the first row and got a front-row view of the bird. He walked up to the stage and told us to get off, and just like that our moment in the sun was over. Talk about fifteen seconds of fame. The curtain closed, and we trudged off the stage.

To say that we were upset would be an understatement. That moment of humiliation was raw. Dave, Sheryn, Michael, and I were pretty angry at Steve for being so stupid and overreacting. But there was nothing we could do about it; what's done was done.

Once I was off the stage and out the back of the hall, I started to feel sick in the stomach. I experienced a feeling of panic, and my breathing was very shallow and fast, and I began to feel faint. I had no idea what was happening to me, but I felt awful. I sat down on the ground, leaned against the wall, and tried to regain control of my breathing. While I was sitting there, I realized something. This wasn't the end of it.

I had forgotten in all the chaos that I was supposed to be singing a solo performance in three songs' time! I felt so sick and anxious and panicked about the prospect of going back out on stage, I decided right then and there that I couldn't possibly go sing in front of all those people and humiliate myself all over again. It didn't matter that it was a different song, that it had no band, and the music was pre-recorded; there was no way I was getting back on that stage in front of the crowd again that night. I ran out from behind the stage while the next group of students performed and told Mrs. Powell in the front row.

Mrs. Powell did her best to convince me to change my mind. She believed I could do it, but any faith I had in myself was completely shot. I walked from the front row to the sound booth at the back of the hall to tell the sound guys my solo number had been cancelled, and I walked out the back door to sit in the cold and dark on my own. My parents hadn't been able to come, so I was all by myself out in the cold, waiting for the rest of the performance to be over.

I felt like all of a sudden, I was right back where I started – no confidence, no friends, and all alone. Of course, it wasn't really true. This was at school; no one from church was there or had any idea what had happened. It was my last week at school for year ten, and after that I was off to Lake Ginninderra College for year eleven, where this moment wouldn't be the focus of school conversation. But in that moment, I couldn't focus on any of that. All I could see was the humiliation I had experienced that I felt would last forever.

Of course, it didn't last forever. School finished for the year, and before I knew it, I was packing my bags to go away for the summer. My parents had helped me organise a summer job back in Loxton, where we used to live, picking apricots on a fruit block. So, the week after school finished for the year, I caught a bus to South Australia.

Arriving back in Loxton was a blast from the past. I hadn't been there for a long time, but it hadn't changed much. A few things had closed, like the drive-in, but otherwise it was pretty much the same as I remembered it. The historical village was still there at the river end of the town, and at the other end of the main street, the big roundabout still had the same three roads connected to it that took you out to the rest of the town.

My parents had organised for me to stay with a family we were friends with from our time living in Loxton, and I had a job on the Williams fruit block picking apricots. After two weeks of this, in the lead up to Christmas, the weather turned hot, and by hot, I mean really, really hot.

Loxton usually had a couple of weeks of super-hot weather every summer, where the temperature was over 40°C every day and got down to 32–36°C at night. During this time, the apricots ripened so fast they had to be picked quickly or they would literally drop off the trees. But it was also much too hot to work through the day. So, I moved out to the Williams fruit block to sleep in a caravan so we could begin work much earlier and finish earlier.

Our day would start at 4:00 a.m. with breakfast, and we were picking apricots by 5:00 a.m. We would work for seven or eight hours solid with a couple of breaks and then knock off for the day at lunchtime. Working after lunch was impossible in that heat with the sun beating down on you.

It wasn't easy to sleep at night either. There was another fruit picker sharing the caravan with me. Shane was a couple of years older than me and had been fruit picking the year before as well. One night when neither of us could sleep, he had an idea.

"Josiah," he said, "how about we put this time to

good use and I teach you to drive? It's not that hard, and out here in the peace and quiet, there are no other cars around, and no one will see us. What do you think?"

While the idea of learning to drive was exciting, it was also a bit nerve wracking too. "I dunno, I'm not sure if I want to try that yet," I replied.

"Well, I am pretty bored," said Shane. "We have got to do something more fun than just lying here in this stinking heat trying to get some sleep!"

I thought about it for a bit. I would be starting driving lessons with Dad when I got back to Canberra, which I wasn't really looking forward to. I could just imagine Dad telling me off for all the mistakes I would make. Maybe it was worth having a go at driving now, so I had a head start when I got back to Canberra.

"C'mon, Josiah," said Shane, "let's go and get the Ute. We can drive on the dirt road out the back near the grapevines. No one will ever know!"

So, we sneaked out of the caravan, jumped in the Ute, and Shane drove us out to the back of the apricot trees so he could teach me how to drive. Behind the apricot trees were about thirty rows of grapevines that were separated from the trees by a dirt road.

Shane drove around behind the trees to the dirt road. We swapped seats, and he began to explain to me how to drive the car. After Shane had explained the basics, he suggested I have a try. I was feeling pretty nervous, but I wanted to learn, and it was something to do when we couldn't sleep. So, I started the engine, put the Ute into first gear, and slowly put my foot down on the accelerator.

Now it was time to panic. As I put my foot on the accelerator and the Ute jumped forward, I was so surprised by the speed of the car that I froze. I was speeding up but not steering, and the car began to veer off the dirt road. It felt to me like everything was happening in slow motion, but it must have only been a few seconds before the Ute smashed into a post holding up a row of grapevines and knocked the post out of the ground. In shock, I took my foot off the accelerator, and the car stalled as the entire row of grapevines slowly keeled over and crashed to the ground.

"Oh, crap, what did you do that for?" yelled Shane. I said nothing. I was frozen in my seat trying to contemplate the consequences of this disaster.

"Get out of the car. I'm driving," he said. So, I opened the door and got out of the car while we both looked at the collapsed row of vines, which represented thousands of dollars' worth of wine grapes. Finally, I managed to say something.

"Do you think we can stand the row back up?" I said quietly. "Maybe if we stand it back up, we could fix it, and no one would ever know?"

"Anything is worth a try," said Shane. "I don't want to lose this job."

So, Shane got into the driver's seat and backed the

Ute away from the vines and back onto the dirt road. He got a shovel out of the back of the Ute, and we began to investigate the posts to see if we could stand them all up again. Grapevines have one large post which is dug deep into the ground about every ten meters or so and then a series of smaller posts that don't hold much weight but keep the wire the vines grow on nice and tight and straight.

Fortunately, only one of the big posts had come out of the ground (the one I hit with the Ute); all the other posts were smaller ones. The next big post ten meters along was leaning over under all the weight it was carrying, but it was still in the ground. When Shane and I stood up the big post at the end of the row I had knocked over, all the other posts stood up straighter as well. So over the next couple of hours, we dug a new hole and fixed the big post on the end, and then we were able to prop the rest of the vine upright so well that we could pretend this had never happened. We put the shovel back in the Ute and headed back to the caravan, where for the first time in quite a while, I was so exhausted, I went straight to sleep.

The next morning, we woke up, got ready for the workday, and headed out to check and make sure the row of vines hadn't fallen over in the night. But it was all good; the vines looked pretty much the same as they had before, and while there was no way I was going to try that again, the owner of the fruit block was none the wiser.

11

More Than a Feeling

As I returned to Canberra at the end of January to get ready for another school year, the one constant thing in my life was our church's youth group and our basketball team. I loved training and playing each week. Even though I wasn't the best player, it was still a good sport for me. I was part of a team and had a sense of belonging to something. Our team had started performing very well over the year, and we were getting better and better, winning games and heading towards the finals.

Our team played on Sunday nights, usually after church was over, but the early game sometimes meant we had to leave during church. I always liked it when people from church came to see the team play, and there was a sense of excitement about the game.

My outlook on life became more positive too. I would talk to Mrs. Middleweek about the things that had happened to me in the past. This is another thing that was amazing that year. She would listen to me and talk to me and kept what I shared to herself. It gave me a chance to talk and get some of my experiences out of my system. The talking helped; she made me feel safe.

But the one thing that was more profound for me than everything else was that I was being challenged about my beliefs about God. The church had become the centre of my social world, but now I was starting to think more deeply about who God is. God had always been a distant idea for me. Sure, I went to church with my family, but if God was real, then I didn't really know who he was. I was scared of the idea of hell and some sort of lake of fire, eternal punishment kind of thing, but apart from being taught what I should believe and think, I didn't really get it. I knew how I was supposed to answer questions about God, but like most kids my age who went to Sunday school, that was all I really knew.

Easter 1988 came along, and our youth group decided to attend Easter Camp. It was a two-hour drive from Canberra to Stanwell Tops on Thursday night before Good Friday. The older members of the youth group and parents packed about thirty of us in cars, and off we went.

When we arrived on Thursday night, it was pretty full on. All in all, there were around 350 young people at the camp with their leaders. That first Thursday night we played a game called capture the flag. All 350 of us were broken up into four teams, and each team had a flag of a different colour to hide somewhere in the campsite. Then your job as a team was to defend your flag while capturing the flags of the other teams. Each team member had a tag, which was a coloured piece of crepe paper wrapped around their arm in their team colour. Your job was to break the tag around the arm of team members from opposite teams. If your tag was broken, you headed to the dining room (which was called the hospital for the game), and you were out for twenty minutes while you had your paper tag replaced.

Each team used different strategies to protect their flag. Our team decided to hide the flag in a safe place, and instead of putting team members around it to protect it, we would set up a dummy camp where we pretended to have our flag while we chased down the other team camps and tried to steal their flags. If you had your tag broken three times, you were dead and couldn't re-enter the game. If your team flag was taken and returned to the hospital, your team was out. No violence was allowed.

It was fantastic. I managed to tag fourteen team members before I got tagged out myself for the third time. In the end, our team won. No one could find our flag. We were the only team to think of setting up a decoy camp.

There were all sorts of activities planned in the camp. There was a giant swing next to the escarpment. First, people were put into a harness, and then four or five people would grab the rope and pull you up so that you would be hanging in the air, in a horizontal position. Then they would launch you from that position, and you would go back and forth. It was quite exciting. There was a ropes course, adventure walks, rock climbing, and a huge range of things to do. I wasn't so sure about the swing myself, so I didn't go up in it. Instead, I helped my friends put people into the harness and then pull the person into position with the rope.

Apart from the fun stuff, there was a guest speaker who spoke to all of us each morning after breakfast for an hour or so, and then we would discuss what he said in small groups with a leader and other campers.

Saturday night was a big event. A band played about an hour of rock music, which we all loved, and then Graeme, the guest speaker, came out and told us about who God is. He was a great speaker, and we were all listening with real interest. Graeme began by telling his own story about how he met God and got to know him. I found this kind of weird. Even though I had been to church most of my life with my family, I had learned about God the Father, Jesus, and the Holy Spirit all my life. But the idea you could get to know God rather than just pray to some distant being who watched us all from heaven took a bit to get used to.

Then Graeme began to talk about Easter and how we could really know the resurrection of Jesus happened. One of the things I remember him saying clearly is that in the time of Jesus, women weren't allowed to be a witness in a court case because they were considered unreliable. While I thought that was a pretty silly way of thinking about women, what Graeme explained was that the first people Jesus appeared to after he rose from the dead were women. If the story was made up, no one would have chosen to make up a story where women were the first to see Jesus and then tell everyone else about it, because in Jesus's time, women were considered to be unreliable. As Graeme continued to explain the evidence for the resurrection of Jesus, it began to dawn on me that this might be really true and not just something I was supposed to know about if I went to church.

As I listened, I thought about what it would mean if I took the resurrection of Jesus seriously for me. The idea that God came to Earth as a person and lived His life on Earth in the same way that we do, experiencing all of life's ups and downs, being killed in an incredibly violent and painful way, and then being raised from the dead by God was a fascinating and compelling story. Especially if that was where love really came from. So far in my life, I hadn't really understood what love was. I thought it was an emotion that people felt towards another person. But Graeme explained that love was a decision to put another person ahead of yourself, and that love could be seen in someone's actions rather than in someone's emotions.

So, we could know that we were loved because God came to Earth and was willing to go through an incredibly painful death so we could be forgiven for our sins and be forgiven. He had taken on the consequences of our own mistakes so we could be free and get to know Him. All the different things I had learnt were beginning to make sense.

Graeme finished his talk, and the band got up to play. The songs they were playing were well-known songs about God, and all 350 of us started to sing along with the band. While they were playing, the atmosphere in the room began to change. I'm still not sure how to describe it, but it was like we were all focused on something greater than ourselves. It felt special to be there. Some of the people were praying quietly, and I really felt like God was somewhere nearby.

The time went really fast, and before I knew it, the band was wrapping up, and it was time to head off to bed. Back in the dormitory I was sleeping in, we started talking about what had just happened. We talked for a long time about what it all meant.

On Sunday morning, I got up early and headed out to sit on the edge of the escarpment. I sat there on the rock and looked out over the edge of the cliff. It was quiet and peaceful, and as I looked out over the valley, I had a sense that God was there with me. I closed my eyes and asked God to show me if he was real, and if he was, could I get to know Him. I sat there for a long time just enjoying the moment.

I don't know how I knew, but in that moment, I felt completely loved and at peace. This was a very different feeling to being accepted by the youth group or my family. For the first time in my life, I felt completely safe and loved. I got this sense from God that I was okay, that I wasn't some broken person who was destined to go through life fighting for acceptance and recognition. The Creator of the universe saw me and knew me, and that was good. The really amazing part was, he knew the real me. Not the person who copied others to be popular or pretended to be someone that others would find interesting and loveable, but the real me, good and bad, and he loved me anyway. While I had no idea how this would impact my life, I knew that things were going to be different somehow.

The moment eventually passed, and I headed into the dining room for breakfast. The rest of the camp was a bit of a blur. Monday morning came along pretty quick, and after a great weekend, we all said goodbye to each other, took plenty of photos, and promised to write letters to new friends. Then, after the traditional end-of-camp hot dogs for lunch, we jumped back in the cars and drove back to Canberra.

Year eleven was getting serious. In Canberra at the end of year ten, we left our high schools and went to college for year eleven and twelve. To enter university, our results from year eleven and twelve counted towards our university entrance score. So, it meant working hard for two years instead of just for one.

As the workload increased, I began to make a few friends with some pretty good students. Ben was a brilliant mathematician and science major and very much into electronics. He loved to build radios and made a bit of money fixing other people's sound systems. Scott was pretty good at most subjects and was good at keeping the conversation going. I enjoyed science as well, but I still had some pretty bad work habits from my earlier school years when I had been discouraged from working hard by the bullying I had experienced.

Ben, Scott, and I used to hang out upstairs during the breaks outside some of the classrooms. A couple of other students we got to know began to hang out with us, and a bit of a group developed.

One of those students inspired immediate interest from me. Her name was Samantha. She was Macedonian, and English was her second language, not that you could tell; she spoke perfect English. Samantha was quiet and hung around the edges of our group to start with, but as she began to relax a bit, we started getting to know each other.

Samantha and I weren't really in any classes together, but each day students had one or two periods free to study rather than be in class. Fortunately, we had the same periods free, so we began to hang out together in the library during our study breaks. I really enjoyed these conversations, and after spending this time together for a few months, we had developed into firm friends.

Samantha was kind, thoughtful, and encouraging. We had several things in common. We both enjoyed watching sport, and we were both from Christian families. We both enjoyed reading, and we even liked the same styles of music.

Samantha talked to me a lot about her family and her life experiences. Her mum and dad were a bit old-fashioned, and her house had a lot more rules than mine did. As our friendship developed, Samantha would confide in me her thoughts and experiences and what was going on for her in her emotional world. I spent a lot of time trying to make her laugh, and when Samantha laughed, it made my heart jump!

College also gave me opportunities to try new subjects I had never studied before. One of the subjects I chose was media studies. It had a theory component where we learnt about the media and how journalism and news worked, and it had a practical component where we got to make films and videos with the VHS technology we had access to in the late 1980s.

The theory part was interesting, learning about how even TV news was designed not to inform the audience but to make sure they paid attention to the advertising was eye-opening. It made me think a great deal about the messages I was taking in through the news, through TV drama, and other media sources that weren't just good stories but were trying to get me to think in a particular way about the world.

The part I loved the most though was the practical work of making films. I made quite a few films during the class that year. I took the camera to State Youth Games and our church camp that year. I filmed the weekend and then edited them into highlights reels I could show at youth group. But I made one film in particular that created some controversy and was also loved by quite a few people at college.

My younger brother, Matt, was still in high school

in year 9, and he was given an assignment for his agriculture class to create an in-class presentation on the anatomy of a chicken and then present his work to his year-nine agriculture class. As a family, we had raised chickens at home since we were young kids, and every year, Dad would kill some of the chickens and pluck them and prepare them for our family to eat. So, I suggested to Matt that we film one of our chickens being killed, and then we could make a video of him showing the anatomy of a chicken as Dad dissected it.

Matt thought this was a fantastic idea, and Dad was happy to help out, so the next day, I borrowed the video camera from school and brought it home so we could create this video. We went out into the backyard, and I set up the camera while Dad selected a chicken. Dad brought the chicken he had caught over to the big log he used for this purpose. He knocked the chicken unconscious and then chopped off its head with an axe.

I filmed the whole process as Dad dissected the chicken and demonstrated all the parts of the chicken on video. Dad knew a lot about agriculture, and his dissection and description of the different parts of the chicken were quite detailed!

Once he was finished, I had about ninety minutes of footage that I needed to edit into a twelve-minute video for Matt to show to his agriculture class. In the media department at school, we had access to an editing machine with computer software to help us edit the video and add a soundtrack to it. Because the video had to be fairly short, I decided to use a music track at the beginning and the end of the video and use text on the screen to show the different parts of the chicken rather than Dad's running commentary of the chicken's dissection.

This is where our brilliant idea began to develop a couple of flaws. I thought it would be great fun to use a song that had been on the radio recently called "Check Out the Chicken" by Grandmaster Chicken and DJ Duck. The song was upbeat, and the chorus was to the tune of the Chicken Dance. It made perfect sense to me at the time, but I hadn't really read the lyrics in detail. I finished editing the video and gave a copy to Matt to take in and show his class the next day.

I wasn't in Matt's class that day, but his presentation became a legend in his school for a long, long time. The "Check Out the Chicken" video of Matt's was regarded as one of the most outstanding presentations the agriculture class had ever seen.

As the video began, you could see Dad knock the chicken unconscious and chop off its head, while in the background the words of the song were,

"Is it a bird? (No)

Is it a plane? (No)

It's Superbird!"

As the axe came down and chopped off the chicken's head a spilt second after the words "It's Superbird" were heard loudly throughout the classroom, the class erupted. Girls were screaming in horror, others were pointing and laughing; the entire class was in an uproar. The video continued with a closeup of the chicken being dissected to the chorus,

"Check the chicken, check out the chicken, chicken, check it out." The class found it impossible to calm down. Matt simply stood there and watched the class's reactions and continued with his presentation.

Verse two didn't help the situation with lyrics like,

"If you wanna be a bird

After everything you've heard

After every single word,

Gotta wiggle when you walk

Gotta wiggle when you talk

Just a little bit."

Unfortunately, during the line, "Gotta wiggle when you walk," Dad was showing the chicken's intestines and moving them about in what seemed to clearly be a wiggling-type motion. Matt's teacher, by this stage, was trying desperately to get the class under control, helping the girls to calm down and get some sense of normality back when verse three started:

"You gotta do the dance

Then you gotta take a chance

You'll be moving like a duck

And you know you're not the first

So you cannot be the worst

The Birdie-Dance."

Of course, to top it all off, in the background at the end of the verse, two live chickens went running through the grass behind Dad, neatly in time with "The Birdie-Dance." The video came to a close, and the teacher tried again to regain control of what was going on. She gave Matt an A+ as long as he promised to never do a presentation like that ever again, and the legend of the "Check Out the Chicken" agriculture presentation was born. I made a few more videos that year, but nothing I did came close to the video I made for Matt in terms of audience impact. Especially when I hadn't even tried to make it funny!

As the year drew to a close, I was beginning to feel like I had found my sense of right place. It can be hard to find, but it's that place where you feel like you're doing things that you're good at and you have some friends around you who care about you, and life made some sense.

I was discovering a lot about myself and becoming more of myself too. Rather than copying the most popular kid, I discovered I had some social skills of my own and a sense of humour that people appreciated. But more importantly, I had learned how to listen to others and help them feel special.

What I had craved as a boy and a young teenager I was learning to share with others, a sense of acceptance and value that is based on the belief that every person is made in the image of God, and therefore they have value because of that one truth. That my authentic self, not the pretend me, was the one that God loved, and that people who loved me wanted to see and get to know.

It made sense to me. Rather than measuring people by their individual characteristics or their popularity, their looks, or how impressive they were, I had learned that the worth of people was determined by God's love for them, not by any person. It was a revolutionary concept.

During all of this, my friendship with Samantha kept growing. Our conversations were epic and went for ages. We would hang out with Ben and Scott and others in our little group at the beginning of lunchtime, but somehow, we would always wind up together, sitting and talking.

There are some obvious things boys do when they like a girl, and I did all of them. When we happened to be in the same room or the same class, I would try to make sure (without being too obvious) that I would end up sitting next to her. If Samantha was interested in a topic, I would find out more about it so I could talk about it intelligently. Basically, I tried to get to know her better and spend as much time with her as I could. I got pretty good at working out my day so we could spend time together.

The cool thing was Samantha also seemed keen to spend time with me. We began to plan our school electives and study classes, so we had the same lessons free each day.

Down the road from college was the Belconnen Mall. The mall had just opened a food court, and there was a café there called Sweet Affair, which sold two of my favourite things in the whole world, vanilla thick shakes and New York–style baked cheesecake. Whenever we had a break, we would walk over to the mall to chat at Sweet Affair. It was during these times our conversations became more open and transparent.

I remember one conversation in particular. Samantha and I were sitting in the food court, and she was quiet for a while, it seemed like she was thinking about something, so I just sat and waited.

"You know," she said, "Sometimes living with my parents is so difficult. They just don't seem to understand what life is like for me. If I do something they don't like they get so upset about it, they try and punish me by not talking to me. Instead of trying to explain to me why they don't like what I have done, they simply ignore me like I am no longer part of the family."

As I sat and listened, Samantha talked about her family. They weren't bad people or anything, they just kept treating her like a child instead of a young adult. It was like she had grown up, but they hadn't kept up with her and were still reacting like she was way less mature than she really was.

We had lots of discussions like this, and as I got closer to Samantha, it became obvious to me that I wanted more than a friendship with her. I would sit next to her in our group during breaks; we would go on walks to the mall or around the lake and chat. She was an awesome girl, and I was becoming smitten.

12

Boldly Going

Towards the end of year eleven, I was asked by the church to join their board of management to represent the youth group's views. The idea was to make sure that the young people in the church were a part of the big decisions the leadership of the church was making. To join the board required a vote of the church members to decide if the person was someone the members of the church wanted as a leader.

This idea was a bit nerve-wracking. I had never been nominated for anything that required a vote before. While I felt like I could make a contribution, I wasn't sure if other people in the church thought the same thing. So, it was a risk for me to put my name forward. What if I didn't get the 70 percent support in the vote that I needed? What if I failed?

One morning as I was leaving home to catch the bus for school, my dad asked me a question. "Who do you think the most effective leaders are in our youth ministry?"

I thought about it for a few moments and then listed a couple of the obvious people I thought of like Barry and Kelly, who already had leadership roles in our youth ministry. Dad looked at me thoughtfully and said, "Josiah, I think you are one of the most effective leaders we have. Leadership isn't about having a title. It's about the way you influence the people around you."

My dad's comment sat with me for a while. I had never really thought about leadership that way. It had always seemed to me that being a leader involved having a title and a set of responsibilities that came along with it.

Eventually I agreed to be nominated. It was the first time I had taken this kind of risk, but it seemed to me that it was pretty rare a person lost a vote for the board, so I had some level of confidence that even if some people thought I wasn't the right person, enough people would tick the box, and I would be elected.

Fortunately, I received over 70 percent of the vote and was elected to the board. But as I thought it through, it seemed to me that Dad was right. Being a leader was more about what you did than having a title or a position.

As I pondered this new concept, I reflected on how I might have helped others in the past. I thought about the friends I had at school now, most of whom liked to talk to me about their difficulties and challenges while I listened. In fact, most of my friendships ended up with me listening while others talked about what they were going through.

I realized was that there are more people like me out there. People who had been through really tough experiences and needed someone to talk to. I had Mrs. Middleweek, who helped me, but what about everyone else who struggled through life? Instead of holding these ideas and feelings inside, like I did for most of my life, people would be much better off if they had a safe person they could share them with.

They really needed someone they could trust, and it seemed to me that I was someone people trusted. This happened even with people I had never met. About this time, I went to the hairdresser to get my hair cut, and I took the opportunity to ask her how life was going for her. In the twenty minutes it took her to cut my hair, she told me about her failing marriage, her frustrations with her kids, and the depression she was suffering from. It was incredible to be in that space and have someone share their life story with me while she cut my hair. It felt good to be able to help, even in just a small way with someone I didn't know.

As year twelve continued, I realized that not only did I have very strong feelings for Samantha, but I was very worried about what would happen if I ever told her about my feelings. I had never asked a girl out before and had never been on a date. The only girlfriend that I had was Tammy back in grade five. All we did was pass notes to each other without even speaking, so not really anything like an actual relationship.

I wanted Samantha as an important part of my life. I loved being around her, having long conversations, going for our walks, and sharing life together as friends, but I desired so much more than that. Here was a person I could imagine spending the rest of my life with. She was fascinating in every way; she was kind, had a soft heart, and really cared about other people.

But I had no idea how to go about this kind of conversation. I wasn't brave enough to talk to her about it face to face. That was way too scary. For weeks and months, I kept silent about how I really felt. I stayed in the friendzone. But I was also aware that this was our last year at college, and who knew what was going to happen after that? Samantha had mentioned some guy called Bradley she thought was pretty nice and might be interested in. Somehow, I needed to share how I was feeling before it was too late. I was sure Samantha had a soft spot for me, but was that more than friendship? It seemed like it to me, but I wasn't the best judge of whether a person was attracted to me. Basically, I assumed they weren't, but because most of the best friends I had in my life were girls, I really had no idea how to tell. Friendship was all I really knew.

One afternoon, as I was sitting in school, I decided to write Samantha a letter. I wasn't sure how she would react, but at least by writing a letter, I wouldn't have to have a conversation about it until she had time to think about it for herself. Knowing Samantha so well meant I was very frightened of being rejected, and my fear of rejection, something I had always struggled with, jumped up like a monster in my heart.

I rewrote the letter about fifteen times. Eventually I managed to put something together:

Hi Samantha,

We are great friends and have lots of fun together. I love the times we spend together, and they are very special for me.

You are an amazing person. You're funny, cute, kind, and incredibly smart. You are beautiful.

I think we could be more than friends.

I would love to go out with you sometime.

Would that be ok?

Love Josiah.

I folded the letter up and put it in my pocket to give to Samantha when I had the opportunity. I was so nervous about it all. I wanted to give it to her when she was about to head off to class, so she wouldn't ask me about it until after she had read it. At the end of lunchtime, with my heart pounding in my chest, I gave her the letter and suggested she read it later, and without looking back, I headed off to maths class.

13

Who Am I?

I didn't see Samantha for the rest of the day. I was so nervous all night, I hardly slept. When I got up in the morning, I almost felt like I was back in grade six all over again. I was afraid of being rejected. I wanted to know what Samantha would say, but at the same time, not knowing what was going to happen felt like it would be better than getting hurt. I was shaking all over as I rode my bike to college. I couldn't think about anything else.

I had two classes before a break, and then we had a study period that Samantha and I both had free together. All through the morning, my mind just churned over and over and over. What would she say? Would this be a great day or a sad day? I had no idea what was coming, but the longer I had to wait and the slower it seemed each lesson went on, the more my confidence slowly ebbed away. By the time our free study period came around, I was starting to prepare myself for the worst!

Finally, it was time, and I headed over to the library where our group usually hung out together. Samantha was sitting in one of the library's meeting rooms already with Ben and Scott, just sitting and chatting. I walked in and said hi to everyone. Samantha smiled at me and said hello and passed me a note. I put the note in my pocket and sat down. I was desperately keen to read it, but I didn't want Ben or Scott to know what was going on, so I sat down and got through about half an hour of what seemed to me at the time pointless conversation. Eventually it was time to go, so I said goodbye to everyone, and I headed off to economics class. I sat down in the back row and opened the note:

Hi Josiah,

I wish you had told me this a long time ago. When I first met you, I was so interested in you. I joined your group just to get to know you. I used to ask Scott where you were so I could find you and hang out with you.

But I am interested in Bradley now. I still want to be friends with you, but that's all.

Samantha

I was completely devastated. I sat in the back of the classroom, and I had no idea what the teacher was talking about. The class went by in a blur. If the teacher had spoken to me, I wouldn't have noticed or cared. The sinking feeling in my stomach was awful. I just wanted to get out of there. When class was finished, I grabbed my stuff and headed for the door. I grabbed my bike and headed for home. I was going to miss the rest of the school day but I didn't care. I had no idea how to talk to Samantha now, and the last place I wanted to be was at college, where I could run into her and have an awkward conversation.

When I got home, I went into my room and shut the door. I stayed there for as long as possible. I didn't want to see or talk to anyone. I put my music on as loud as possible and let myself experience the pain of rejection all over again. While I was in my room, I decided the best way forward was to pretend this had never happened; I needed to hide my wounded self away from the world again. At school the next day, I wouldn't mention it or discuss it with Samantha. I would simply pretend it had never happened. But deep down inside, I knew that our friendship would never be the same again.

The next day, I headed off to college and pretended it had never happened. I buried all those feelings inside myself and determined that Samantha would never know how much I regretted not telling her earlier during all those weeks and months when we both liked each other, but I was too scared to speak up. I blamed myself for being so timid and fearful.

Samantha and I never had a single face-to-face conversation about it except for those two notes. If you had observed us from the outside, you wouldn't know it had ever happened.

We were coming to the end of the year, and I was trying to work out what I was going to do in the future. Should I go to a university? Should I get a job? Or should I do something else? While I was trying to figure all this out, our church invited a team from a Christian Youth Work organisation to run a ten-week course helping us learn how to reach out to young people and teach them about being a Christian.

Part of the course was designed to help the students think about what their true purpose was. The purpose God had given them to fulfil during their lifetime. As I thought about this, it seemed to me that my purpose might be to help other young people like me.

When the course was completed, we got together as a group to think about what we could do in North Canberra to connect with other young people and build friendships with people in need. During the discussion, I suggested that we could run a nightclub on Saturday nights. We could invite people to come, and instead of alcohol, smoking, and drugs, it could be a safe place where people could just hang out. We could run it in North Canberra, so people didn't have to go into the city to go out on a Saturday night. It would give us a good opportunity to get to know the people who came and give us an opportunity to introduce them to what we believe as Christians.

As we discussed the idea, the rest of the leaders decided it was something worth exploring. So, we invited a number of other churches to get involved, and we started working on it. We had to fundraise for sound and lighting equipment and all the other resources we would need. We negotiated to hire the local community centre on a Saturday night as the venue and made sure we had all the insurance and legal stuff covered as well.

I found the entire process inspiring. I was already thinking about what I want to do with my life, and here was something I could see myself doing for a long time. I'd been thinking about going to university and training as a primary-school teacher. I was becoming more convinced that helping young people like me was what God wanted me to pursue.

College was almost complete in November when we opened the nightclub. It was called the Rockpile. We had a professional DJ, non-alcoholic mocktails, and we had advertised the launch all over North Canberra. The first night, around 160 people attended. They were all aged between fourteen and twenty years. It was a new project, and people in town were very excited about it. The second week, we had two hundred people come in. Over the next few months, it kept growing.

The Rockpile was one project, but I knew I needed to learn more if I was going to be effective as a youth worker. Fusion were advertising a diploma in youth and community work in Sale, Victoria, and I felt God saying to me that this would be a good next step. It was a six-month live-in course for people who were serious about becoming youth workers, followed by a six-month placement in one of Fusion's youth work centres somewhere in Australia.

I thought it was really interesting, and I talked to my parents about it. They were not very keen on the idea. They wanted me to go to university first, so I had a backup qualification before I went into youth work or church work. But I felt strongly about completing the course, so I applied for it.

I was accepted into the course, and in January 1992, I packed my bags and left for Sale on this new adventure. I had left Samantha, my friends and family behind, to do something for God I felt called to. It was a compelling feeling to look forward to what I could do to help others. If I could make a difference in their lives, then maybe God could do something good with all the hard things I had experienced.

EPILOGUE

Josiah's story didn't end here. Josiah is a survivor, a young man who made it out the other side of childhood trauma and bullying, finding his true self as a person created by God to make a difference in the world.

Josiah's story continues today. He has dedicated his life to helping others discover who they have been created to be. He invests his life, his energy, and his learning in the lives of others as a tribute to the God he trusts and believes in, and in recognition of the people who have helped him become the man he is today.

But this is only one person's story. Thousands of young boys and girls are bullied and traumatized in our schools every day in my country and in yours. Every single one of those lives is equally valuable, made in the image of God and precious in His sight.

As we grow and learn, there are many voices that ask for or demand our attention. Josiah grew up with voices that said, "Prove that you are good enough." Or

"You should be ashamed of yourself." One of the biggest voices Josiah grappled with said, "Nobody really cares about the real you." But underneath all these often very noisy voices is a still, small voice that says, "You are loved, my favor rests on you." That's the voice we need most of all to hear, the voice of God. To hear that voice, however, requires some effort; it requires solitude, silence, and a determination to listen. That's what prayer is. It is listening to the voice that calls us loved and valuable, the God revealed in His creation and in those who truly follow Him and His Son, Jesus.

Maybe in reading Josiah's story, you will find your own voice; maybe you will be inspired to reach out and lift up a person who desperately needs someone to believe in them, like Mrs. Middleweek did for Josiah. Maybe the God of the universe can inspire you to touch the heart of a child who needs to be loved and inspired to be who they have been created to be.